For fifteen years now *Perry*  acknowledged to be the wor fiction series. Originally pu in Germany, the series has now appeared back and paperback in the States.

Over five hundred *PERRY RHODAN* clubs exist on the Continent, and *PERRY RHODAN* fan conventions are held annually. The first PERRY RHODAN film, SOS FROM OUTER SPACE, has now been released in Europe. The series has sold over 200 million copies in Europe alone.

THERE IS NOW A BRITISH PERRY RHODAN CLUB. Send SAE to Dave Taylor, 15 Alwyn Gardens, Upton by Chester, Cheshire, who will send full details by return.

Also available in the PERRY RHODAN series:

KURT MAHR

Perry Rhodan 27:
Planet of the Gods

Futura Publications Limited
An Orbit Book

An Orbit Book
First published in Great Britain by Futura Publications
Limited in 1977
Copyright ©1973 by Ace Books. By arrangement with Arthur
Moewig Verlag.

DEDICATION

This English edition dedicated to
ROBERT MOORE WILLIAMS
Author of *"Land of the Golden Men"* . . . and Many Others

Series and characters created and directed by Karl-Herbert
Scheer and Walter Ernsting, translated by Wendayne
Ackerman and edited by Forrest J. Ackerman.

ISBN 0 8600 7965 1
Printed in Great Britain by
C. Nicholls & Company Ltd
The Philips Park Press
Manchester

Futura Publications Limited,
110 Warner Road, Camberwell,
London S.E.5

Chapter One

CONFUSION TO THE ENEMY

Perry Rhodan had just announced "We're eight light-days from 221-Tatlira and outside the range of the Springers' observation." His tone was casual, calm, as he sat with his back to the console aboard his ship the *Stardust*.

But the peculiar reddish eyes of the ice-and-fire alien from Arkon burned even redder in anger as Thora approached Perry Rhodan, scoffing: "Beyond their observation, you say! But to reach here you had to pass through two hypertransitions. Surely the Springers would be more than inept if they hadn't noticed."

Ignoring Thora's angry outbreak, Rhodan turned to his co-pilot. "Bell!"

Reginald Bell knew what was expected of him by his friend and commander. He snapped to attention for the Arkonide woman's benefit and reported in official tones: "Our structure sensors registered transitions at a rate of 55 per hour. Presumably Springer ships blasting off and landing on their base, Tatlira II."

Rhodan turned his head toward his severest critic. "Well, Thora? Satisfied?"

Thora was visibly exasperated to be treated in such a cavalier fashion and her indignation mounted swiftly. "I know exactly what you're thinking!" she exploded. "You assume that your own transitions went unnoticed among so many others. But what if you're mistaken."

Rhodan shrugged his shoulders. "Then we'll make another quick hytrans farther away to a place where the Springers won't suspect us to be."

Thora relaxed her antagonistic tone. Her voice softened to an almost pleading whisper. "Why won't you listen to my proposal, Perry? Why don't we fly to Arkon and ask the Galactic Imperium to come to our aid?"

Perry leaned forward in his executive chair so far that he almost reached Thora's hands. His eyes sought hers earnestly. "Let me explain the situation to you," he said, and there was no hint of condescension in his voice. "We learned from a Springer renegade that the patriarchs of the Springers convened their Great Conclave on the second planet of the sun Tatlira 1012, light-years from Earth. Four of our mutants – Marshall, Kakuta, Ishibashi and Yokida – were smuggled onto the renegade captain's ship, bound for Tatlira II, in order to convince the Springers, by applying their parapsychological powers, that an attack on Earth involved the risk of their own ultimate destruction.

6

"However our plan met with only partial success. One of the patriarchs decided to subject the outcast captain to a forcible brain analysis. We know that Marshall managed to prevent the critical cerebral probe by killing the traitorous captain and averted the menace of the patriarchs by the blast of an atomic bomb.

"But we still don't know how well Kitai Ishibashi, the Suggestor, has succeeded in making the patriarchs believe the bluff that we on Earth are armed to the teeth with irresistible weapons. We've no assurance that the Springers won't launch their offensive against Terra in the next few days – or hours, for that matter – in spite of our past efforts.

"But we have to know and we'll soon find out. We don't have time to fly to Arkon, to negotiate for weeks with the Galactic Council, perhaps with negative results. We must stay here and get in touch with at least one of our four mutants.

"I appreciate that you've made your offer out of a generous wish to help Terra and not as a scheme to return to your home. Nevertheless you'll have to agree that we simply don't have the time to accept your proposal."

He drew back his hands and got up. He took a few random steps, suddenly stood still, turned around and smiled at Thora. "Besides," he said softly, "Four of my men are stranded out there on Tatlira II. Barring an absolute necessity I will not permit them to fall into the hands of the enemy. So far we're not in such desperate straits as to leave four of our men in the lurch!"

* * *

Tako Kakuta contemplated his present predicament with unkind expletives. Here he was with his parapsychological potential of teleportation enabling him to transport himself anywhere within 30,000 miles as long as he was familiar with the outstanding features of the locality and was constrained from making use of his gift. Instead he moved closely above the uneven grassy plain toward the town in the vicinity where they had landed.

They – Tako Kakuta himself, John Marshall the telepath, Kitai Ishibashi the Suggestor, and Tama Yokida the telekineticist – were invisible due to the deflector screens around their spacesuits powered by a small built-in generator.

After the mutants had started to influence the patriarchs' thinking by implanting fanciful ideas in their minds about the formidable defenses of Terra the old patriarch Etztak thwarted their operations at the Great Conclave. They were forced to kill Levtan, the renegade who wanted to ingratiate himself again with his people, as well as slay most of the patriarchs in the ensuing showdown. Finally they fled.

They flew over a vast ocean and landed on this island where time seemed to have stood still. The city they were approaching was situated only six miles from the place where they had come down. It consisted of high but narrow frame houses built so closely together that there were no streets or only very narrow ones running between them.

The city stretched out along the ocean and possessed a natural harbour that presented an unusual sight.

Sailing ships!

Sailing ships of all sizes and of many varied types but none of them more advanced than those on the seas on Earth at the beginning of the 18th century!

And all this existed in a world the Springers regarded as their personal property and where they had come to meet in an important conference.

On Goszul's Planet.

Tako Kakuta adjusted the speed at which he moved toward the city. He didn't intend to land at the harbour before he had familiarized himself with the layout of the city. He was about three miles away from its western end. The little antigrav aggregate in his transportsuit held him at a constant height of 15 feet above the ground.

The terrain gradually inclined toward the city. It was covered with grass broken by low irregular outcroppings. Tako had concentrated all his attention on the city before him so that he failed to notice the gray shadow gliding rapidly across the land.

The object throwing the shadow raced

through the air at considerable speed about 1500 feet above the ground. It had a circular cross section and displayed the general shape of a lens as could be seen by observers watching it execute a skilful turning manoeuvre 10 miles west of the city. It turned back toward the city, losing height and speed and giving off a slight whistling sound.

The whistling was the first sign of the threatening danger which Tako perceived. He turned around and discovered the lens-shaped craft a few hundred yards behind him.

He saw that it was one of the auxiliary ships which the big Springer spaceships carried on board by the score or even hundreds. His first impulse was to go down to the ground and seek cover. On second thought he realized that no cover could be more effective than the protection provided by his deflector field.

He slowed down and hovered motionlessly in the air. The auxiliary ship came gradually closer. It didn't fly in a straight line but on a zigzag course as if searching for something.

Tako suddenly shuddered. What could they be looking for in this deserted prairie unless they pursued him? At the same moment Tako became aware of his danger it had already become acute. The occupants of the auxiliary ship seemed to be certain of their target. A concentrated pale-green energy beam shot out from the outer rim of their craft.

It missed Tako by less than 15 feet and streaked into the ground, blackened it and raised a cloud of vaporized grass. Tako reacted quickly in the only sensible manner: he focused on the spot where Marshall, Ishibashi and Yokida waited for him and performed a hurried teleportation jump.

Due to his hasty imperfect concentration Tako landed about 600 feet from the temporary place where the companions he left behind had settled down. The terrain was hilly. It looked as if a high mountain had been covered with soil almost up to the top. Steep rocky peaks towered from the grassy surface to a height of 300 feet. Dust and soil swept up by winds had managed to gain a precarious hold on the steep walls of rock during the years and airborne grass seed had grown a dense cover of vegetation on the flanks of the peaks, changing their rugged contours to softer lines. The opposite side from the prevailing winds on Goszul's Planet, however, still dropped off almost vertically in a dangerous precipice.

Soon after their arrival the four fugitives had discovered a spacious cave on the west side of the highest hill and taken refuge. From there Tako Kakuta had started out half an hour earlier to look at the city.

When Tako materialized again on his return he first gazed at the sky. The lens-shaped Springer ship was nowhere to be seen. Probably, Tako thought grimly, they're now racking their brains how it was possible for me to disappear so suddenly.

11

Now he began to worry about the still unexplained fact that the Springers had been able to spot him so easily although he was invisible.

He concentrated his mind on John Marshall's name. He was certain that the telepathic Marshall could pick up his thoughts over the distance of 600 feet between them. He endeavoured to give a mental description of the incident which had just taken place. He wanted them to avoid the great danger to which they were exposed should they rush out of the cave. They would make perfect targets for any other Springer ships scrutinizing the fields from high altitudes. Marshall would be in a position to warn his friends.

Tako then floated back to the cave, taking time to observe the surroundings. Although the ship of the Springers failed to show up, Tako didn't draw the premature conclusion that they had lost his track.

He reached the cave, switched off the deflector field and recounted the attack. When he noticed the consternation on his comrades' faces he added: "Of course it could be nothing but an accident!"

Marshall smiled. "Thank you for your tranquillizer pill, Tako!" Then he shook his head. "No, we can be quite sure that it was no accident. I've been afraid all along that the Springers have the means of detecting our transportsuits. The suits contain a generator to supply the energy for the deflector screen, antigrav field and the protective shield against gunfire. All these aggregates together

12

produce a considerable amount of scattered radiation and it isn't very difficult to pick up this radiation and pinpoint the source of its origin. Iı this assumption is correct the transportsuits are no longer useful to us. On the contrary, they attract the Springers. We'll have to . . ."

"But we don't know what the critical distance is!" Yokida interjected anxiously. "If they can make us out from a distance of less than 300 feet it would still be preferable to wear the suits because of the protective shield."

Marshall raised his eyebrows. "If . . ." he answered with emphasis. "We don't know. Perhaps they can spot us from a hundred miles." He shook his head and stared with a vacant look. "No," he murmured, "I'm afraid we'll have to discard the suits and. . . ."

Marshall suddenly threw up his head and gazed at the ceiling of the cave. Yokida wanted to say something but Marshall hastily waved him off. "Quiet!"

Two seconds later he got up. "They're above us," he said calmly. "Rather close at that. I can almost distinguish their individual thoughts. They know our location within 50 feet. Quick! Take off your suits!"

Tako stripped off his suit and ran to the opening of the cave. Without sticking his head out of the exit he saw the auxiliary ship hovering 150 feet high above the grassland. In an instant he was ready with his plan.

He returned to the others and demanded: "Give me your suits!"

They looked at him questioningly.

"Quick – no questions!"

His team mates picked up their suits and handed them to Tako who had to carry the full weight of the heavy outfits. All aggregates were switched off. At the moment the Springers could receive virtually no impulses from them.

"Wait here!" Tako told them. "I'll lead them astray."

Marshall called to him: "No, it's too dangerous. You won't . . ."

But Tako had already disappeared. When he materialized again he could only guess how far away he had moved from the cave. He had leaped too swiftly to get his bearings. The Springer ship was out of sight.

He had landed not far from a slim rock, jutting up high. He ran to seek cover behind it. There he put down his heavy load and donned one of the suits. He turned on the generator and waited.

* * *

Back at the cave Marshall posted himself behind the entrance and kept a sharp lookout. He glanced up at the Springers' ship.

"They don't move," he commented. "If we had more efficient weapons than our little impulse beamers, we could bring them down."

"Maybe if we fire all together ..." Ishibashi started to suggest. But Marshall shouted at the same time: "They're flying away!"

Ishibashi and Yokida rushed forward. They saw the auxiliary ship gather speed and fade away southwest in the direction of the ocean.

"Tako has done it again!" Marshall exclaimed admiringly.

* * *

Tako Kakuta saw the ship coming.

It proceeded close above the ground in the same zig-zag course which he had observed earlier. The instruments with which the Springers tracked down the radiation of the transportsuits didn't seem to be very efficacious.

Tako waited till the craft was about to circle the rocky needle. Then he jumped, but only 300 feet.

The pilot seemed irritated. He kept flying around the rock without detecting the three transportsuits carefully hidden by Tako but eventually he locked on to the radiation from the suit Tako wore.

The ship discontinued its circular path and approached him again. Tako waited till it had once more come in a critical range and took another leap. This time he bounded twice as far away.

He felt certain that his impact shield could absorb such shots as could be fired from the auxiliary ship. But it was also certain that the impact shield would in that case require additional energy from the generator which would have to be diverted from the deflector field, thereby rendering Tako visible again. This Tako wanted to avoid in the interest of his own health, especially since the automatic target tracker was capable of holding him in sight as long as desired once it had locked on to an object like him. If necessary he could have been kept pinned down until reinforcements with weapons strong enough to pierce his protective screen arrived on the scene.

This time the pilot reacted in a different manner. As soon as he received the new signal he broke off the search at the previous spot and closed in on him.

Tako repeated his jump and reached the shore half a mile away. The Springer ship kept close on his heels.

Hiding behind a cliff Tako slipped out of his transportsuit but left all aggregates running so that the Springers received the impulses with un-diminished force. Then he teleported himself a few miles out over the ocean, carrying the suit in his arms. He appeared again a few feet above the water's surface, fell down into the water and dropped the suit. He swam away and watched the white outfit slowly sink into the ocean.

Then he transported himself back to the place where he had deposited the three other suits. He completed his job, covering up the transportsuits with heavy boulders and making sure that it was impossible to detect them, all the more so as the residual radiation from the aggregates which had been turned off would be damped out in 15 minutes, furnishing not even the slightest impulse to the Springers.

He performed another hop, getting within half a mile of the cave and vaulted with a final effort in the midst of his companions.

"Everything's fine," he grinned. "Right now they must be scratching their heads trying to figure out what we're doing at the bottom of the sea."

He related briefly what he had accomplished and Marshall slapped him on the shoulder. "Thank you very much, Tako!" he said simply.

Tako shrugged his shoulders. "You're welcome. But what are we going to do next?"

Marshall pointed out of the cave. "We'll walk to the city," he proposed. "We can't stay forever in this queer place!

There were no objections.

*   *   *

The constantly rotating beam of the *Stardust*'s sensor system struck a metallic object at the limit of its effective range, was reflected and made a green blip appear on the observation scope. The automatic monitoring system was, following Perry Rhodan's instructions, on constant alert and reported alarm stage No. 3 in a fraction of a second.

Rhodan was at once informed in the Command

Centre. He kept in touch with the Rangefinder Section and watched the identification of the object.

"Distance 42×10^6 miles. Velocity 11.4×10^4 miles per second. Component in our direction . . ."

Seconds later: "Object measures less than 300 feet, sir!"

Another few seconds later: "The object is cylinder-shaped, sir! Length 250 feet, diameter approximately 30 feet."

And finally: "Movement apparently directed by steering. The object is a spaceship."

It had been quite obvious to Rhodan. The craft seemed to come straight from 221-Tatlira. A Springer ship from the depth of space.

Rhodan called the Defence and Security officer. "Sensor shield?"

"Functions in perfect order, sir! The alien could have located us already without the shield. We're continuously receiving impulses from him."

The field of the sensor shield surrounding the *Stardust* was as new as it was effective. The device prevented the reflection of wave beams up to very high intensities and above this limit it was capable of confusing all approaching opponents by creating a minor reflex indicating a distance of millions of miles when the *Stardust* was only a few hundred thousand away.

Rhodan ordered alarm stage No. 2 when the alien ship had come within 600,000 miles and he accelerated the *Stardust* under the protection of the sensor shield. During this manoeuvre, which was partially controlled by the automatic steering pilot device, Rhodan asked two of his corps, Ras Tschubai and Pucky, to come to the Command Centre.

Tschubai took a shortcut. He was a teleporter like Tako Kakuta and suddenly appeared in the Command Centre. A few moments later Pucky, the most capable member of Rhodan's Mutants, entered through the hatch door after he rose on his hindlegs outside the door, pushed the button and made Rhodan open the door.

Pucky had no trouble at all to transport himself by teleportation from one deck of the gigantic spaceship to another but he still found it a little difficult to move around like a human being and he was not quite satisfied with his progress.

He was a cross between a beaver and a mouse, covered with reddish fur and three feet long including his stubby tail. Pucky belonged to a species of semi-intelligent creatures endowed with natural telekinetic gifts whom Rhodan had encountered on his trip to the planet Vagabond. He had clung to Rhodan, who had trained him in a special process adapted to his undeveloped brain. Rhodan succeeded in expanding the great potential of Pucky's conscious mind and in awakening more of his hitherto hidden parapsychological talents. Pucky had become an accomplished telepath and teleporter. He mastered several languages and joined the Officers Corps of the New Power as a mutant.

There were some people who considered Pucky a freak and disapproved of naming him to the rank of officer. But Pucky knew how to convince everybody very quickly that he was not only an excellent mutant but above all an amazingly clever tactician.

Rhodan smiled at him and after the hatch was closed he said: "I've got a job for you both. It concerns the hostile ship over there."

* * *

The little vessel was a reconnaissance craft, only lightly armed but possessing great acceleration and manoeuvrability.

The commander of the ship was Frernad who belonged to the mighty clan of the Frers and his vessel was named *FRER LXXII*, a figure which looked big and ugly to Frernad since the spaceships of his clan were numbered according to their size which meant that the *FRER LXXII* was one of the smallest crafts.

Old Etztak was responsible for Frernad's orders to search for foes far out in space. Etztak had been in a scrape on a far distant world with an enemy whom he now was stalking and in Frernad's opinion Etztak suffered a bad case of jitters.

Frernad hated this mission but he executed it faithfully nevertheless. The sensor beams swept the field constantly. However, so far they had registered nothing except a few slowly drifting masses of rocks. Utterly bored, Frernad stared at the little instrument dial which registered the distance from the place he had started from by measuring the amount of energy used up. The thin indicator line of light was creeping slowly to the 10 light-day mark on the scale.

"Two more hours," somebody remarked. "Then it'll be over!"

Frernad turned around and raised both hands as a sign of agreement. "I'll sing praises the moment we land again!" he smiled grimly.

The Command Centre of the *FRER LXXII* was small and was occupied by three men. The crew of the vessel consisted of 18 men in all.

Frernad wanted to say something, when the operator of the rangefinder hastily spoke up. "A reflex!" he called. "There . . .!"

Frernad made a morose gesture but got up and walked over to the scope. The technician in front of the instrument pointed to the screen where a big bright spot was quickly fading away.

Frernad was vexed. "What do you mean, it just appeared and it's gone again?"

The man raised his hands but before he could say anything a strange loud voice came from the control panel: "Don't let it bother you, friends! I caused that reflex!"

They whirled around and stared at the man who suddenly stood beside the console. They had never seen anybody like him. He was tall – almost as tall as they – but his skin was black.

He laughed when he saw they were frightened

21

and showed his glistening white teeth. The space-suit he wore had an unfamiliar cut and his helmet was open as he talked to them. He spoke impeccable Interkosmo although in somewhat of a monotone.

All this was noted only incidentally by Frernad. The main question to which he could find no answer was: *How did the man manage to get in?*

Frernad opened his mouth to ask him but the black started to move so quickly and purposefully that Frernad was fascinated by his actions. He watched how the stranger dexterously pulled a spherical object from a pocket of his outfit and turned a screw or a switch which extruded from the top of the ball. Then he looked up and studied Frernad and his two men very intently.

"What are you doing?" Frernad finally inquired. "Who are you and what . . ."

That was as far as he got. With a suddenness he had never experienced before in similar situations, he lost consciousness. There was not even time enough for him to recognize what happened to him nor could he see whether his two companions fared better than he. He simply keeled over.

Ras Tschubai gazed at the three unconscious men with a happy grin. Then he closed the helmet of his spacesuit although the filters he had inserted in his nose were enough to protect him from the narcotic gas released from the round bomb.

However, he wanted to be prepared for any difficulties in case the gas didn't pervade the ship fast enough and he took the extra precaution to be ready for trouble.

With his foot Ras Tschubai pushed the ball he had put on the floor toward the ventilator shaft. The constant circulation of the air would carry the odourless, colourless gas everywhere inside the ship in the shortest time as it was not filtered out.

His job was finished. The crew of the small Springer ship would remain unconscious for four hours. This was all the time Rhodan needed for his plans.

Ras Tschubai jumped instantly back to the *Stardust* by teleportation.

*   *   *

"Now it's your turn, Pucky," Rhodan said gravely. "Take your stuff across!"

Pucky nodded in a human manner. He gazed for awhile at the observation screen on which the Springer ship was shown as a little point as the *Stardust* kept a constant distance of 20,000 miles from it. Then he looked at the equipment which he had piled up around him – weapons, microcoms and other emergency gear.

A heavy disintegrator vanished from the stack as if it had never been there. One of the microcoms went, followed by a case of miscellaneous supplies. The pile had disappeared in three minutes – transported telekinetically with precision on board the small enemy ship.

Pucky made a wry face and intimated a grin with his incisor tooth. "I'm leaving now," he lisped amiably.

Rhodan's eyes made a last, quick check of the little creature's spacesuit which was specially made for the mouse-beaver. "O.K.!" he approved. "Do a good job! Marshall and the others must be located under all circumstances. We want to know what they've accomplished among the patriarchs. And besides, we want to rescue them!"

Pucky gave no answer. He stared straight ahead and departed the same way the equipment had vanished.

He appeared again in the main corridor of the *FRER LXXII*. He quickly determined that Ras Tschubai's gas bomb had indeed put the entire crew out of action and found a spot where he intended to spend the time till they landed on Goszul's Planet. It was a small empty compartment at the end of the corridor and Pucky had no way of finding out what purpose it served.

Pucky stowed away his baggage in the compartment and took out the hypno-weapon Rhodan had provided him with. With the weapon in hand he systematically visited each room in the ship and administered treatments to each member of the crew one at a time, thereby safeguarding the *Stardust* and himself in the most effective manner.

Finally he reached the Command Centre where Frernad and his two aides received hypnotic instructions.

Next Pucky studied with great interest the rangefinder screen. He watched the hairline sweeping across a space sector as the search antenna rotated. Yet he noted no reflex whatsoever. The *Stardust* and the three heavy cruisers farther out in space remained undetected.

It had been Rhodan's contention – with which Pucky agreed – that a few reflexes were registered on the scope during the last half hour when the protective screen of the *Stardust* was deactivated for a fraction of a second to permit the jumps of the teleporters and the telekinetic transportation of the gear through the field. These protective shields were five-dimensional fields and presented a barrier for the teleporters moving in a five-dimensional continuum.

Pucky considered this to be an unnecessary flaw and tried to figure out a method of maintaining the sensor shield uninterruptedly when a teleporter left the ship.

After satisfying himself that everything was ship-shape he retired to his chosen hide-away, made himself comfortable among his bundles and waited for things to happen. He had already arranged with Rhodan at the outset that no microcom message would be sent unless something had gone wrong.

The effect of the narcotic gas released by Ras Tschubai's bomb wore off as suddenly as it had begun.

Four hours after Frernad's hair-raising experience of seeing the sudden appearance of a black stranger the Command Centre of the *FRER LXXII* came to life again.

Frernad got up at the same time as his two men. Without wasting a look at his surroundings Frernad walked to the rangefinder console and stared at the grid. At the same moment the technician reached his post and sat down in front of the screen and the third man also returned to whatever he was doing when Ras Tschubai interfered.

". . . and it's gone again?" Frernad repeated in the same surprised tone the words he had spoken just before the weird incident had occurred.

The man at the rangefinder set raised both hands. "I said it was very big and clearly visible!"

Frernad laughed angrily. "You're letting a stray reflex confuse you, Sifflon. It was probably only an electro-magnetic interference which caused the reflex."

"Well," Sifflon murmured, "after all, I didn't claim it was a hostile ship."

Frernad went back to his controls. With a bored expression the third man who had attentively listened to the conversation took up his work again where he had left off. He waited to take over the controls when Frernad wanted to be relieved.

None of them had retained the slightest recollection of their mysterious encounter with Ras Tschubai. By carefully selected hypno-impulses Pucky had also corrected the error caused by the momentum of the flight during which the *FRER*

LXXII had moved a considerable distance in space after Ras Tschubai had entered the ship.

Not even the empty bomb container which Ras Tschubai had pushed in front of the ventilator shaft aroused suspicion. The third man discovered it as his eyes wandered around, picked it up and showed it to Frernad who didn't know what to make of it. He told the man to throw it away.

Pucky had taken another precaution. Not once did it occur to the crew during the entire flight to look into the little compartment at the end of the main corridor.

Two days later the *FRER LXXII* had reached the farthest point from Goszul's Planet on its prescribed course and reversed its direction. Pucky had inspected the instruments on a visit to the Command Centre. Furthermore, he was able to read the thoughts through the wall of his little room whenever someone came close enough.

He knew that it would take 10 days before he could set foot on Goszul's Planet.

Chapter Two

IRONIC DISCOVERY

Halfway to the city they encountered a wagon drawn by animals resembling horses.

After they had taken off the transportsuits, they wore again the clothes they had first put on aboard Levtan's ship in order to be inconspicuous. Thus their exterior appearance was virtually indistinguishable from crew members of a Springer ship. Even their beards, trimmed in the latest style worn by the Springers, had sprouted in the meantime.

It was questionable, however, whether the concept of a spaceship was familiar to the inhabitants of this island. One would normally expect that people using sailing ships had no knowledge of spaceships and would be unable to recognize spacemen.

"We'll have to try it out," Marshall had said. "We won't get anywhere hiding all the time."

So they kept silently walking toward the rumbling wagon as it approached them on the gentle incline.

A single man sat on the wagon bench, holding

the reins in his hands like an old-time farmer on Earth. The man was startled when he saw the four strangers. He halted his animals and shaded his eyes in order to see them better.

Marshall and his three companions, who had the strong light of 221-Tatlira at their back, could see that the man was frightened.

I hope he at least understands Interkosmo so we won't have to learn his language, Marshall thought.

They stopped when they had reached the cart. The man was so scared he had not dared to move. He was still holding his hand above his eyes.

"*Zul bel!* Good fortune today!" Marshall offered the most common of the Springers' greetings.

The man stared at him with wide open eyes. As if suddenly jolted, he dropped his hand from his eyes, leaped from his bench to the ground and fell on his knees, lowering his head. Marshall heard him mumble some words he couldn't understand.

"*Plek, staron!* Please get up!" Marshall requested.

The man obeyed instantly. Marshall was greatly relieved to find out that he obviously understood Interkosmo.

"Look at me!" Marshall demanded next.

The man, who seemed to be fairly old, looked at him with fear in his eyes.

"*Moro?*" Marshall asked. "What's your name?"

"I . . . I . . ." the old man stuttered in a rasping voice, "I am Vethussar Ologon, Lord!"

"We're on our way to the city, Vethussar," Marshall continued.

Vethussar bowed. "It'll be a great honour for the city if you visit it, oh Lord, and I would consider it a favour if you would let me offer you my dirty wagon."

Marshall looked at the cart. It couldn't have been cleaner.

"You may!" he replied. "We're very much obliged for your kindness."

"I'm your servant, Lord. There's no need to thank me."

The oldster let Marshall and his friends climb onto the vehicle. Marshall moved leisurely and took time to probe Vethussar's thoughts. So far he had been unable to notice anything except the tremendous shock the old man felt since they met and it had overshadowed all conscious thoughts. Gradually the terror subsided and feelings of suspicion mixed with admiration emerged.

Are they really . . . ? Vethussar thought. *Do they exist at all as they say, these . . . ?*

The expression was not clearly sensed by Marshall and he was unable to ascertain its meaning. It occurred twice and Marshall tried to comprehend it while Vethussar laboriously turned around his wagon and headed down the way to the city.

After Marshall had noted the same expression a few more times in Vethussar's mind, he decided to translate the word as Gods. At the moment he couldn't think of anything else that came closer to its true meaning.

Marshall turned around to his companions and let them in on the result of his probings. He spoke English and was certain that it wouldn't make Vethussar suspicious. After all, Gods were supposed to be intelligent enough to speak more than one language.

He noticed, however, that Vethussar seemed puzzled by the foreign language.

Slowly they approached the city. Vethussar had frequently turned around during the last few minutes as though he wanted to say something. Marshall perceived his desire to ask a question. "*Vak!*" he encouraged the oldster. "Go ahead. What do you want to know?"

"Forgive my curiosity, oh Lord!" Vethussar burst forth, "it's the first time for your humble servant to set eyes on a God. As you're so benevolent to me, I wish to know if you can teach me about the Land of the Gods."

Marshall was surprised to see the alacrity with which the old man changed from breathless fright and respect to undisguised curiosity. He seemed mentally very alert and apparently he refused to believe –

"You know, Vethussar," Marshall replied in a casual tone, "it doesn't look much different from here. The grass and the trees are green and the water in the oceans is blue as long as the sun shines.

31

However, there are vehicles there which are much faster than your wagon and others which can fly through the air, even ships in which one can travel to the stars."

Vethussar seemed greatly impressed. Only Marshall was able to recognize the little spark of scornful suspicion in the back of Vethussar's mind. The oldster's next question quickly followed: "And why did you travel on foot, Lord?" He had spoken in a tone of deep humility.

You rascal, Marshall thought, more amused than angry, *you never believed in Gods and now you want to play a trick on a God!*

Marshall faced an important decision. He could choose to give the native some evasive answer but it was a good bet that Vethussar would resist accepting a subterfuge. On the other hand he could explain to him that they were no better than Vethussar and that the only difference was due to their higher development of technology which transformed nobody into a God.

He decided in favour of the second way. "Stop, Vethussar!" he called.

Vethussar was jarred. He held back the animals and looked around anxiously. "Yes, Lord!"

Marshall pointed forward. "Look at that tree!" he ordered.

Vethussar turned around again and stared obediently at the tree. Marshall raised his little impulse-beamer and fired a short burst at one of the lower branches past the oldster's shoulder.

The branch was blasted from the tree and turned into smoke and ashes as it fell. Little flames lapped the grass but were quickly extinguished in the humid soil.

Vethussar trembled. But Marshall wasn't finished yet with his lesson. "Now look to the left where the road turns!"

Marshall gave Tako Kakuta a sign. Tako had already grasped what Marshall had in mind. He suddenly vanished from the cart and emerged at the same instant at the spot Marshall had pointed out and waved to them.

Vethussar was terrified and uttered a grunting sound. Marshall didn't have to tell him to turn around. He convinced himself with his own popping eyes that the stranger standing over there was the same who sat in his carriage less than a second ago.

Tako quickly returned to his seat in the same extraordinary manner in which he had departed.

Vethussar broke out in sweat and when he was finally gripped by a strange, unseen power which pulled him up from his bench and whirled him through the air, he began to scream. The telekin Tama Yokida had lifted him as high as the treetops, turned him a few times around his axis and let him gently float down again on his wagon.

Gasping and wailing Vethussar collapsed on his seat, Marshall let him carry on for awhile, then he shook him by the shoulders. "Listen to me Vethussar!"

Vethussar meekly ceased his moaning and looked apprehensively at Marshall.

"We're no Gods, Vethussar. Nobody has ever seen a God. We're simply people like you and those living in your city or elsewhere. We know a little more than you, that's all. You don't have to be afraid of us. On the contrary, we want you to have some compensation for your trouble taking us into town and you may tell us what reward you'd like to get."

He watched as the oldster hesitantly took in his remarks and slowly began to trust him. Vethussar kept staring attentively at Marshall for awhile. Then he straightened up, took the reins and got his animals going again. Bumping and creaking the wagon slowly rolled toward the city.

"We're going to be in trouble," Marshall said pensively to his friends. "We're bound to create a big commotion among the people in town. They'll also believe we're Gods. Vethussar first became alarmed by our clothes and when I used the greeting of the Springers – 'Good Fortune Today,' which is considered by the islanders to be a greeting among Gods – he was quite certain of our identity. Of course, we won't have to repeat the imprudent greeting but our uniforms will make us suspect. I suggest we send Vethussar first alone into town to pick up some other clothes for us. Any objections?"

They shook their heads. Marshall turned to Vethussar and explained his request. "Unfortunately," he admitted at the end, "we don't have any money to give you. But perhaps there's something else you'd like to have?"

Vethussar had a strong sense of honour. Marshall had trouble convincing him that his offer of payment wasn't meant to be an insult. "Where I come from," Marshall pointed out, "it's the custom to pay for such services."

Feeling already half-reconciled, Vethussar relented. "It's the same with us but not among friends," he agreed.

Marshall could read in his mind that he was sincere. Vethussar was touched by the frankness with which they had treated him. From now on he was the most trustworthy ally Marshall and his three companions had on Goszul's Planet.

About a mile from the earthen wall which surrounded the city on land, Vethussar left his wagon behind with his new-found friends and promised to be back with appropriate clothes before nightfall.

* * *

Szoltan, the pilot of the auxiliary ship, who had conducted the weird search during the past hour, made his report to the assembly of the patriarchs – or rather to what was left of it after the ambush.

"The search has brought no results. Several impulses were received but the source of origin changed so erratically that the pursuit turned out to be a major problem. Eventually the impulses shifted to the ocean and the last one we registered came from a depth of 10,000 feet."

This meagre result was all Szoltan had to report and he was certain that he would receive no praise for his performance from the patriarchs. He was afraid they might transfer him.

However Szoltan's fears proved to be wrong. He got a prompt reply from the patriarchs. "Turn over your ship to your second-in-command and proceed to Saluntad, the capital of the island. Before you enter the city, however, you'll have to contact our agent a-G-25 who'll provide clothes for you such as are worn locally so you won't draw undue attention. Use extreme caution as a-G-25 is the only man we have in Saluntad. The inhabitants are Goszuls who are still backward. We presume that the fugitive crew members of the *LEV XIV* are headed for the city after they somehow got rid of the equipment that gave their presence away by throwing it in the ocean. Agent a-G-25 will assist you. He is very influential in the city."

Szoltan breathed free again. He had expected much worse.

He took off in his ship and landed in the vicinity of the city. His co-pilot took over the controls and before leaving he sent out a radio signal to a-G-25. The agent answered the call and was told where to find Szoltan and to bring him some plain and inconspicuous clothes.

Then the ship lifted off and moved in a northerly direction rapidly gaining altitude. Szoltan waited patiently for the sun to set in one or two hours and hoped that a-G-25 would not keep him waiting too long.

* * *

The garment Vethussar brought looked just like his own: a rough shirt held around the waist by a rope and baggy trousers tied around the ankles, a pair of sandals and a cloak without sleeves.

Apart from the simple pattern, the garments didn't seem to be those of a poor man. The conclusion drawn by Marshall was that Vethussar was no pauper.

Vethussar was pleased to hear his new friends express their thanks. With a smile he announced: "I've brought you something else!" He pulled a small tin can from the deep pocket of his cloak and held it up. "Vetro!" he said cryptically.

Marshall hastily tried to discover what the stuff was. But Vethussar was so intent on watching his friends' reaction that his thoughts didn't betray his secret.

"It's incredible," Marshall exclaimed feigning joyful surprise. "Give it to me, my friend!"

Vethussar handed him the little tin can. Marshall opened it and saw that it contained an ointment of reddish colour.

"It's especially for you," Vethussar beamed. "The others would probably attract no attention."

At the same moment Marshall was able to read

in Vethussar's thoughts why he had brought the cream. Vetro was a preparation for darkening the skin to give it the reddish colour of the planet's natives. To judge from Vethussar's thoughts, the little can must have been worth a small fortune.

Marshall thanked Vethussar and let him rub the cream on the permanently or temporarily exposed portions of his skin. To be on the safe side, Yokida, Kakuta and Ishibashi got the same treatment.

By the time they were ready, the sun had already set. Darkness fell quickly upon the land. They climbed back on Vethussar's wagon and a few minutes later passed through a breach in the earthen wall which could be considered to be the western gate to the city of Saluntad. It was the only place where they could hope to find some means of travelling back north across the ocean.

If this proved to be impossible, they'd have to place their hope for leaving the island again in Tako's special talents.

* * *

Pucky distinguished himself from humans in one essential respect: he didn't have the ability to be bored. His race had an inborn urge to play. It was not playing as such they enjoyed most of all but the delight of tricking an unwilling partner in their games.

In the beginning Pucky had almost made a shambles out of the *Stardust* and its hapless crew

38

since his inherent sense of play knew no limits. Such rules as there were had to be taught later and now Pucky knew what games he could afford to play as, for instance, in the present circumstances.

Five of the remaining 10 days had elapsed. The *FRER LXXII* was going back to Goszul's Planet at 98% the speed of light.

One day Pucky telekinetically transported into his little chamber one of the men who had come within 15 feet of the wall and relished to his heart's content the puzzled face of the poor trapped fellow. Then he made him forget, via his hypnotic influence, the weird sight by which he had been frightened and he began to sound him out for information about conditions on Goszul's Planet.

Thus he combined business and pleasure. He collected information on the world where his mission was taking him and had some more fun listening in on the arguments between the evicted man and his fellow crew members who wanted to know where he had been so long while he steadfastly claimed he had never left his place.

The general hypnotic prohibition preventing them from looking into his chamber remained unaffected by his little game.

* * *

Vethussar's prominent status in the city became apparent when he showed his friends his home

By the light of crackling torches on the way to

Vethussar's domicile they were amazed to see the house fronts in Saluntad which resembled so much the buildings erected in the western half of the Earth at the beginning of the 17th century.

Vethussar's residence was an exception. It was actually much more than a house. It was a veritable palace!

It stretched more than 150 feet along a narrow street and its exterior was a horrid example of bad taste. But Marshall felt Vethussar's unrestrained pride and he professed to be greatly impressed.

Vethussar led his guests through the portal and once inside it became clear how rich Vethussar really was. The interior of the large building was lavishly decorated and its ornaments were far less gaudy than the outside.

Vethussar was delighted by the sincere compliments paid by his invited guests. He insisted that Marshall and his companions stay with him as long as they could, all the more because they lacked money. Marshall finally accepted for himself and the others.

Vethussar showed each one into a room. They had trouble convincing their host that there was no need to have a personal servant for each of them but they were unable to talk him out of assigning a servant to the four of them together. "I've never had such highly eminent guests as you," Vethussar said with cheerful eyes, "and you shall be treated as the notable personages you are."

His friendliness would have seemed exaggerated

to Marshall except for the fact that he could read in the back of his host's mind that Vethussar expected some benefits from his hospitality, arising from the extraordinary talents of his guests.

* * *

"O.K., let's get together on where to go from here," Marshall proposed the next morning. "Who's got an idea?"

Tako Kakuta had already been at the harbour before the city had gone to sleep. "I've looked at the ships," he said, "and talked to a few people. The ships look as seaworthy as can be but they take four weeks to sail 3000 miles when the winds are normal. If it comes to the worst we could travel by ship. However none of the captains will agree to embark on a journey to the north where the Land of the Gods is situated, which instills the greatest fear in them. Kitai would have to exert his influence on the captain and the most important officers – perhaps even on the whole crew to prevent a mutiny."

Marshall agreed. "The distance from here to the shore of the northern continent is about 2500 miles. If we figure that we make good time, the voyage should take a little more than three weeks, which would suit our purpose. We've got to keep in mind that only on the northern continent can we find a possibility of leaving this planet and returning to Rhodan. We must capture a spaceship from the Springers. On the other hand it will be better for us if a few weeks go by between our caper at the Great Conclave of the patriarchs and our next action."

Marshall rose. "I'll talk with Vethussar at the next opportunity," he concluded. "As far as I can tell, Vethussar derives his prosperity from a far-flung trade across the seas. The chances are that he owns a few ships and can make some favourable arrangements for us."

Vethussar entered a few minutes later, his face looking rather annoyed. Marshall understood that he was upset about some visitor. "I'm very sorry," Vethussar began after saying Good Morning, "but Honbled has found out that I have guests in my home and now he came over to offer you the blessing of the Gods."

"Who is Honbled?" Marshall asked, since Vethussar could think only of his dismay.

"Honbled is the highest priest in town," the old man replied. "In my opinion he is also the greatest fool but I can't tell him that because he enjoys enormous prestige around here since almost every-body believes in his Gods."

Marshall laughed. "Why don't you let him come in?" he suggested. "I don't mind his blessings."

Vethussar sighed in relief. "Fine, then I'll bring him in."

They waited a few minutes and their host returned with a man who was so fat he could hardly squeeze through the door. His skin was pale

42

and his beard very sparse. The man could not be much more than 30 years, measured by Terranian standards.

"This is Honbled," Vethussar announced curtly and unfriendly.

Honbled didn't let it disturb him. He raised his left hand and put it gently on Marshall's forehead. "May the Gods bless you, my son!"

Then he repeated the same procedure with Tama Yokida, Tako Kakuta and finally with Kitai Ishibashi. After that he awkwardly sat down on an easy-chair amidst much groaning.

"I've heard you came from afar," he began the conversation without beating about the bush.

"Yes," Marshall answered curtly and began to probe the thoughts of the priest.

"May I ask from where?" Honbled inquired.

Marshall took a stab in the dark and replied: "From the mountains." He didn't know enough about the topography of the island to be aware whether mountains existed or not. He could tell, however, how amused Vethussar was by his prevarication.

But what of Honbled himself? "From the mountains?" the priest wondered. "Do you belong to that hardy tribe of mountain people who brave wind and weather and live in total abstinence to the joy of the Gods?"

Marshall became more and more puzzled. Tako Kakuta seemed to sense his confusion and gave the reply in his stead. "Well, we don't practise quite as much moderation as you people down here seem to think," he stated boldly. "We do alright. We celebrate our holidays and our women have the reputation of being the most beautiful in the country."

Honbled looked disappointed. "It will grieve the Gods to hear this," he said, as if his feelings were insulted. "The Gods love it if their creatures live with temperance. They punish those who revel in debauchery."

The Japanese seemed to enjoy the conversation. "I didn't say we're debauched," he countered. "I only wanted to correct the impression that we're a sanctimonious bunch of narrow-minded fanatics who despise the good life."

Vethussar was utterly delighted.

"And we get married," Kitai contributed with a serious face.

"And sometimes we take a snort," Tama Yokida chimed in.

Honbled got up indignantly. "I can see that you still suffer from the rigours of your long trip." He tried to save face in the embarrassing situation. "If the Gods are willing, I'll come back to visit you tomorrow to learn more about the people in the mountains."

He waved with his left hand and left the room. Vethussar followed him, grinning from ear to ear.

Marshall jumped up as soon as the door closed behind the two. "He must have a block!" he panted. "I can't make out his thoughts."

44

Tama Yokida shook his head. "No, he doesn't have a block," he asserted calmly.

Marshall looked at him perplexed. He knew that Yokida had beside his telekinetic gift also the ability to perceive the outlines of invisible objects no matter how small they might be. Therefore he would have been able to recognize any mechanical device in the brain of the priest.

"What is it then that he's got?" Marshall bellowed.

"He's got nothing at all," Yokida smiled. "But he's something – he's a robot."

Chapter Three

THE MEN FROM *LEV XIV*

Agent a-G-25 returned much sooner than expected. Szoltan saw him walking down the street from the second floor of the building where the agent lived. Szoltan smirked as he watched the subservience with which the passers-by greeted Honbled at the same time and admired the ingenuity of the scientists who had constructed such a humanoid being.

The corpulent figure entered the house through a narrow door leading over a few low steps to the street. A few minutes later he appeared before Szoltan, panting like a real human being. He pulled a handkerchief out of his soiled priestly habit and wiped his brow. "It's them!" he exclaimed. "Without the slightest doubt."

"You mean the men from the *LEV XIV?*"

a-G-25 stretched out his hands in a gesture of uncertainty. "How should I know?" he asked. "I couldn't question them about it, could I?"

Szoltan became angry. "Then how do you know they're the ones we're after?"

"Because there are no telepaths among the

islanders," Honbled replied. "But one of those four definitely was a telepath. I could feel how he tried to reach my brain."

Szoltan smiled a little derisively. Honbled's brain was spread out over his whole body. It was a hodgepodge of fast and slow switch elements, databanks, printed circuits and control taps for electronic measurements.

Szoltan was far from satisfied. "What did they tell you?"

Honbled related the conversation and added angrily: "And they poked fun at me."

Szoltan threw up his arms. "What if they happen to be right? If they're really mountain tribesmen and have telepaths in their midst?"

Honbled was still sweating profusely. "There could be telepaths among the people in the mountains," he admitted and concluded after a pause calculated for effect, "but there are no mountains on the entire island!"

* * *

"Is he an agent of the Springers?" Marshall asked tersely.

The others knew as much or as little about it as Marshall and it was therefore a rhetorical question.

Nevertheless there could hardly be anything but an affirmative answer. Nobody on this world except the Springers were able to build a robot. And if there was such a technical marvel in Saluntad, it must have been a Springer robot.

Granted this surmise to be correct it was also a fair guess that Honbled had visited them solely for the purpose of finding out whether they were indeed the fugitives on the loose.

"This will affect our plans," Marshall declared. "If the Springers know that we're in this city, they'll also watch the harbour and soon learn when we take a ship. Once we're at sea it'll be an easy matter for them to lay their hands on us."

"H'm," interjected Yokida. "We could unmask that priest. All we'd have to do is to slit open his belly in public for everyone to see what kind of a tin soul they revered as a priest."

"And what would we've gained by doing that?" Marshall challenged him. "Nothing! The Springers would still keep an eye on us. We don't even know whether Honbled is the only spy they've got in town. No, it'll be much better to play along with Honbled till we can be sure that he suspects us. As soon as we find out what he's going to do about us we can act accordingly."

They all agreed on Marshall's proposal. Vethussar was told nothing about it. He was happy that somebody had dared to ridicule the priest.

* * *

"It'll work," a-G-25 assured with emphasis,

"I'm sure of it and it'll be very simple, too. Such a heinous crime will enrage the population. It won't make any difference that he's the richest ship-owner on the island. We'll make everything look completely natural without technical aids. In order to be useful here I must live in peace and the population must be pacified. If we start demolishing houses with disintegrators and subdue the people by hypnotic methods, it would mean the end of peace and good faith. We should never forget that we've made the Goszuls retrogress by involuntary means and we don't know what memories of the time of their superb technology have been relegated to their subconscious mind "and retained."

Szoltan conceded that he was right although it was a blow to his vanity that he had lost in a discussion with a robot. "Then what do you propose we should do?" he asked gruffly.

"We'll plant the incriminating evidence," a-G-25 said quickly. "Then we'll rouse the temple wardens and march on his house. We'll be joined by many people on the way. We'll surround the house and demand that Vethussar surrender what he stole. He'll laugh at us and then we'll break into his house and force Vethussar to let us arrest the four men from the *LEV*. They won't be able to escape because we'll have the house immediately surrounded. Vethussar won't resist us because he knows that we can punish him by death for his transgression."

Szoltan turned up the palms of his hands as a sign of assent.

* * *

Marshall awoke from his sleep and looked around. A fire of smokeless wood burned low in an iron brazier in the middle of the room and he could see Tako Kakuta sitting at the door in its glimmering light.

Since Honbled had paid them his visit they stayed together in one room and took turns at keeping watch. "Tako!"

The Japanese turned around. "Yes?"

"What happened?"

"There's nothing unusual. All's quiet."

Marshall sat up and listened. A peculiar sensation had caused him to wake up. If it could have been heard, or seen, or touched, Tako would have been sure to notice it. However it was no . . .

There it was again!

A thought impulse revealing terrible anguish. And another from a second brain.

Very far away, Marshall thought. *Could be in the right wing of the house.*

He woke the two other men up. "Something is going on there," he said apprehensively. "There are at least two people over there who feel dreadfully frightened. Let's go take a look!"

They had looked at the layout of the house the previous day. It was arranged in a simple and

50

symmetric pattern. They tiptoed in the darkness along the main corridor to the right wing and the impulses received by Marshall became clearer.

Pointing to a barely discernible door a few feet down the corridor on the right side, he whispered. "In that room!"

They advanced cautiously along the wall and heard some scraping noises through the door. A suppressed but angry voice said something in great haste.

Marshall followed the content: "I wish we had finished this already! What sacrilege! The Gods will punish us for this notwithstanding Honbled's dispensation. Let's hurry up and leave!"

Marshall was satisfied. He saw a narrow strip of light through the crack under the door coming from the illumination inside the room. Marshall sneaked up to the door and motioned Tako to follow him. Tama and Kitai remained a little behind.

Marshall kicked in the door and all four rushed into the room which was lit by a few flickering candles. The two men inside screamed in terror.

They had been busy emptying a large wooden box and placing its contents on a shelf in the back of the room.

"Hold 'em!" Marshall called out.

Then he examined the shelf and saw his suspicions confirmed. Vethussar used the little room as a kind of treasure chamber. Precious articles of every description were displayed on the boards of the racks and the contents of the box were just as valuable as the objects collected there. They were little figures of gold encrusted with precious stones in their main features. The box had contained about 20 such statues. If gold and precious stones had a value on Goszul's Planet comparable to that on Earth, the two men had lugged in a considerable fortune in the wooden box.

Now what? Marshall pondered. He couldn't interfere if Vethussar wanted to supplement the artifacts in his treasure chamber at night.

But then there was the anxiety the men so strongly exhibited. Why were they frightened to such a degree that it excluded all other emotions and thoughts in their minds?

"Kitai! Question them!"

Kitai faced the two men and forced one of them to look at him. "What are these figurines?" he demanded.

It was impossible to give false answers to Kitai's questions. Kitai Ishibashi possessed such strong suggestive powers that nobody could resist his will.

"They're the images of the Gods from the main temple."

"Did you steal them?"

"No."

"How did you get them?"

"Honbled, the high priest, gave them to us."

"Did he tell you to put them here?"

"Yes."

Marshall intervened. "It's enough, Kitai. Skip it now!"

52

Kitai's questions and his suggestive influence had caused the man to overcome his fear and to think about the matters relating to the interrogation. Marshall not only found out what had happened but also learned what was going to take place very soon.

Marshall looked around. Some of the boards of the cabinets were fastened to the corner posts with leather straps. Marshall removed all articles from one of the boards and took off the leather straps. "Tie 'em up!" he said tersely. "One of you has to call Vethussar. Hurry up!"

Tama Yokida darted away. The two intruders had scarcely been bound and gagged when Yokida returned with Vethussar. Nearly stupefied, Vethussar blinked at the flickering candles.

"Kitai!"

The Japanese knew that they had no time to lose. Vethussar was still drowsy from sleeping and it could have taken an hour to explain the intricacies of the plot without some coaching by suggestion but Kitai had to say a word only once and the oldster grasped the situation and realized that a disastrous storm was brewing over his head.

"These two men have told us," Kitai concluded, "that Honbled and his temple guardians will be here one hour past midnight to accuse and arrest you. This gives us only an hour and a half. What are you going to do about it?"

Vethussar was at a loss to think of ways how to

foil his tormentor. The devilry of the priest – who surely would have succeeded without the vigilance of his guests – exasperated him so much that he was unable to express two related thoughts.

"Well, it's up to us," Marshall stated in English. "The oldster is quaking in fear."

He turned to Vethussar. "Where is the main temple?"

Vethussar described its location.

"Tako, you'll have to move the evidence out of the house. Our strategy will be most effective," Marshall explained in Interkosmo so the old man could understand him too, "if the stolen images are returned to their rightful place. Then we can denounce Honbled, charge him with slander and kick him out."

Vethussar clapped his hands enthusiastically.

Marshall continued in English. "On the other hand it'll be a question whether the robot can be dissuaded from his scheme by all this. I don't believe he'll simply turn tail if he can't find the statuettes. He might try anyway to overpower us, so keep your finger on the trigger!"

Tako performed a trial jump to the main temple. Since Marshall had defined the whereabouts of the main temple even more precisely by extracting additional information about the surroundings from the mind of Vethussar, the jump was accurate within a couple of feet.

Tako landed in the dark inner sanctum of the huge temple building. Behind him, close to the portal, a small sacral fire was burning and two attendants stood near the door but didn't notice Tako.

Tako found the altars from which the golden idols had been taken and returned to Vethussar's house.

With three more jumps he restored the stolen goods and finished his job shortly after midnight without having attracted anybody's attention. Vethussar was thus rendered impregnable to Honbled's calumnies and he thanked his friends exuberantly.

In the meantime Marshall had already given some thought to the best way of extricating himself safely from the net of the Springers drawing closer around them without having to abandon his present favourable position.

He had 40 minutes to devise a plan.

* * *

Vethussar sent some of his own men out to gather information and they returned with the news that Honbled harboured since yesterday a guest nobody had ever before seen in town.

Marshall received the information half an hour past midnight. He was certain Honbled would have the house surrounded before he proffered his accusations in public.

Therefore Marshall and his friends left the house to watch the blockade outside. In great haste and with reinforcement by suggestion they gave Vethussar some instructions which he was to transmit by a messenger to the man in the harbour whom it concerned.

Marshall said in conclusion: "It's possible, my dear friend, that we won't be able to enjoy your hospitality much longer. It'll all depend on the situation. In case we don't see you again, we'd like to assure you that we're deeply grateful to you. You've proved to be a real friend and we hope you'll remember us."

Vethussar was very touched. "Don't even mention gratitude," he declined. "I'm the one who is indebted to you. You've saved me from death and the loss of my honour!"

There were only 15 minutes left to the time Honbled had set for moving in on them. They bid a quick goodbye and sneaked out into the vast, park-like garden behind Vethussar's palace.

They moved cautiously with Marshall in the middle because he concentrated his attention on extraneous thoughts.

He touched Kitai Ishibashi, who was crawling ahead of him and held his leg when he perceived the first impulse. "Somebody is ahead of us, a little to the right," he whispered.

A few seconds later they heard the bushes rustle. Honbled's men moved into position for the siege.

Marshall was jolted when he got the first expression from a highly developed brain: "A few more minutes and the patriarchs will get their prisoners back and my troubles will be over!"

* * *

Honbled and Szoltan had each chosen their roles. Honbled as priest and accompanied by his assistants, assumed the task of public accusation. Szoltan had hurriedly hired some helpers and impressed on them that nobody could be allowed to escape from the encircled house.

One hour after midnight Szoltan had positioned his men. He had selected a place for himself where he was alone. Impatiently he watched the minutes tick by on his chronometer.

He was startled when he heard a crackling in the bush near him. He tried to see in the darkness and snarled angrily: "Didn't I tell you that you have to remain at your assigned places?"

The bush to his right was parted and two crouching figures flitted toward him. "No, you didn't tell us a thing," a strange, deep-throated voice replied.

Szoltan was terrified and before he could overcome his shock of surprise he was dealt a strong blow to his head which knocked him out instantly.

"We got him!" Marshall whispered.

Kitai and Tama came up from the rear.

"Over there!" Marshall pointed farther away.

The two Japanese carried the unconscious Springer through the bushes and dense groves to

the rear wall of the park. Tama used his telekinetic powers to lift the body over the wall and
kept it floating in midair on the other side until
they had climbed over the wall. Tako Kakuta
followed them and Marshall was last. "All is quiet
now," he said, "but the big ruckus will start in a
few moments.

A few steps farther down in a side street leading
along the wall a wagon with two draught animals,
which had been provided by Vethussar at their
request, was waiting for them. The unconscious
Springer was loaded into the wagon. Kitai, Tako
and Tama sat down so they could keep an eye on
him without being seen from outside. Marshall took
the driver's seat, tugged the animals and drove
them down to the harbour.

* * *

Vethussar took his time when he heard the fat
priest banging against the portal with both fists. He
waited till his servant came to his bedroom and
reported: "Honbled, the high priest, is at the door.
He's irate."

Vethussar pretended a yawn. "Tell him to come
back tomorrow. I'm accustomed to sleeping at
nights."

The servant trembled like a leaf. "He won't take
that for an answer, sir. He's got nearly all his
temple wardens with him and they allege that
you've committed an abominable crime."

Vethussar popped up in his bed. He played his role with great verve. "I? The most faithful servant of the Gods – a crime of desecration?"

He leaped out of his bed with agility and shouted to the servant: "Bring me my cloak, quickly ... and a torch!"

Outside Honbled resumed drumming against the door. With the cloak draped over his shoulders and the burning torch held high in his hand the old man finally pushed open the wide portal and planted himself with his feet spread apart in front of the rotund priest.

"What kind of nonsense are you telling these people?" he yelled at him. "Who committed a despicable sin?"

But Honbled was not to be intimidated. "You!" he screamed back, pointing at the old man. "You've robbed the temple of 14 idols to enrich yourself. You've affronted the Gods!"

"Who dares to accuse me?"

"Two guardians have seen you and one of your servants as you were carrying a heavy box out of the main temple."

"It's a barefaced lie!" Vethussar retorted.

"No!" Honbled cried out. "Let us search your house and we'll soon find out where you're hiding the divine statues."

Vethussar laughed scornfully. "First lead me to the temple and show me which idols are missing!"

"So that your servants can meanwhile hide the treasures somewhere else?" Honbled sneered.

But Vethussar quickly countered. "You can leave some of your men around the house, then you'll be sure that nothing will be concealed from you."

The crowd behind Honbled raised concurring voices. Honbled had no interest in a delay but he knew that Szoltan was lying in wait behind the house and decided to give in to Vethussar's demand.

With smoking torches the crowd – growing bigger by the minute – marched down the street to the main temple.

"Open the gate!" Honbled shouted from afar, and the two attendants who had remained behind at the holy edifice obediently opened the high portals.

"You with the torches, line up along the walls so we'll have some light." The huge temple hall was lit up by the yellow light of the smoky torches.

"And now," Honbled announced with a mighty voice, "I'll show you the altars which have been robbed and defiled by this miscreant. Look there . . . !"

He was startled. Nothing was missing from the altar of the God of the Sea although he had instructed his two men to strip it first because the idol was priceless.

". . . or there!" he went on.

But the Fish God was at his place – with his golden scales and glittering eyes of precious green stones.

"Or there!" Vethussar mocked him, swinging his torch around, "or there . . . or there!"

Honbled's mechanical innards registered and classified the new situation and caused the exterior of his body to express human reactions of surprise, disgust and fear.

"Where are the stolen images? What am I supposed to have taken from here? It's all there! Tell me what did you expect to find in my house?" Vethussar taunted.

Honbled's powers of deduction worked rapidly. He considered all possibilities including the one that Vethussar had smelled a rat and brought the statues back in time. But the logical sector of his brain declined to translate his cognition in words and remit them to his vocal chords since nobody in the crowd seemed willing to believe another word from him.

Vethussar's righteous exhortations inflamed the people. Those without torches drew closer around the old man and the priest and the others came from the walls and lit up the scene.

"The priest has lied," Vethussar exclaimed. "He has lied to plunder my treasures!"

"The high priest!" the crowd raged.

And so Honbled was done for. The crowd set upon him with a vengeance. Agent a-G-25 was a powerful machine and able to beat off the first attackers. However, the mob had meanwhile grown to more than a thousand raving people and there was nothing left to do for Honbled but to emit an emergency call and to let the events take their course without further resistance. A hail of blows and kicks damaged his inner mechanism and immobilized him. His last reaction was to close his eyes.

A minute later he was believed to be unconscious or dead and the mob withdrew from its victim. Honbled's enormous bulk prevented his real inner substance of plastic metal from becoming exposed. Thus the citizens of Saluntad were spared the metaphysical shock of seeing a disemboweled robot.

Vethussar had already departed from the crowd some time ago and returned to his home. He spread the news of Honbled's downfall and chased his knaves out of his house with the help of his servants.

After finishing this job with great gusto he retired to his private quarters. He made a servant light a few torches and watched the water clock slowly measuring the hours. It had been refilled four hours before midnight and the water's surface stood at the sixth hour line.

As it passed the line three cannon shots thundered from the port. Vethussar smiled in satisfaction and extinguished the torches. Going back to his bed he thought: *that Fafer is a dependable man.*

* * *

The only difficulty they experienced on their way to the port was caused by the two draught animals.

Marshall had so little time to find out before he left how to handle the team that more than once the animals went left when he wanted them to go right and vice versa. Nevertheless they reached the harbour in half an hour.

It was easy to recognize the ship they were looking for. The *Storrata* was the only ship which showed more than the usual night illumination at this time and where obviously some work was in progress.

Marshall drove the wagon to the gang plank leading from the lowest of the three decks to the pier and they were immediately noticed from up above.

"We've been sent by Vethussar at this hour of the night!" Marshall called.

These were the exact words of the message arranged by Vethussar's messenger with the captain of the *Storrata*.

"Come on up!" somebody called back.

They hauled the still unconscious Springer down from the wagon, carried him across the gangplank and boarded the ship.

A man in a uniform with splendiferous colours greeted them. Marshall probed his thoughts. *Astonishment, curiosity and a little anger* that he was ordered to put to sea at this late hour.

"I'm Fafer," said the man. "Be welcome!"

Marshall expressed his thanks. "I'm very sorry we're causing you so much trouble. We had occasion to render your master a very significant

63

service and he's anxious to show his gratitude. I'm convinced you'll be rewarded by Vethussar if you'll help us to leave the island quietly."

Fafer's mood perked up considerably, as Marshall could gather.

"I'll do my best," the captain assured them. "Come with me! I'll show you to your cabins."

Close to the stern of the ship, narrow steps led to the middle deck. Fafer walked toward the stern and opened at the end of the gangway a row of doors leading to lavishly furnished rooms which astounded Marshall and his friends.

"The window over there," Fafer explained, "has the widest view aboard ship. Because the stern is slanted from the upper deck to the water, one can look up as well as down."

This was a convenient advantage and the other rooms had similar wide windows.

Fafer politely inquired if his guests were satisfied with their accommodations and took leave after he had been reassured that they were as luxurious as any place they had visited.

"I'll have to perform an intricate manoeuvre," he excused himself. "The tides will change in about an hour. If the ebb doesn't carry us out far enough the tide will throw us back."

Fifteen minutes later three cannon shots shattered the quiet night and soon they watched the view from the window beginning to move. The lights of the harbour glided back and the dark outlines of other ships drifted by.

64

The *Storrata* left port.

* * *

The following morning a few people casually asked Vethussar about his guests. Marshall had predicted that something like this would happen and had told Vethussar not to make a secret of their whereabouts.

Consequently Vethussar informed the inquirers that his four friends had sailed away on the *Storrata*. Because their mission had been so urgent Fafer had agreed to set sail during the night. No, not to the Western Isles, to the Southern Continent.

Marshall knew that the first contact had been made and that the flow of information had begun.

* * *

Marshall's second medium was the prisoner Szoltan himself.

For good reasons Marshall had refrained from searching his captive or taking anything away from him. Marshall was certain that Szoltan carried some device enabling him to give signals for tracing him.

This was precisely what Marshall wanted. After the Springers had learned of their presence in Saluntad there was no point in delaying their return to the Northern Continent. Their main reason – to let things calm down after their first bout with the patriarchs and to wait for them to relax their vigilance – was no longer valid.

However, in order to cover the distance of 3000 miles in a shorter time than it was possible on a sailing ship, he needed the Springers themselves. They had to be informed where Szoltan and his captors could be found.

Everything had worked out just as Marshall could have wished. The ship had cleared the harbour before the tides changed and with a fair wind in its sails in the morning the *Storrata* set course to the south.

Chapter Four

PUCKY'S TRIUMPH

Goszul's Planet was a name which had been in use for a short time – short compared to the old history of the people now called Goszuls.

The Goszuls called themselves Gorrs and their world Gorr. They were Arkonide settlers who had come many thousand years ago to this sector of the Galaxy from their homeland Arkon in huge spaceships. Thus the Gorrs belonged to the same race as Thora and Khrest to whom Perry Rhodan owed the phenomenal rise in technology by the New Power on Terra.

Certain climatic and physiological influences on the planet Gorr had caused first a slowdown and then stagnation of the civilization and technical developments of the settlers. About 1500 years after they had established themselves on their new world the technological trend had reversed itself completely and was sliding back to a stage where objects which had been used for centuries were no longer manufactured because they had forgotten how to produce them.

Of course this development came about at a very

slow pace and the people of Gorr would have remained at a relatively high level of technology if the Springer Goszul had not discovered their world and decided to spur the backward trend of their development by artificial means.

The Springers had methods available to accomplish this. They were a race of traders who had no homeland of their own. They enjoyed a trade monopoly and were widely if unofficially regarded to be the most advanced group in the Galaxy because they travelled around more than all others The Springers as a race were related to the Arkonides and politically they formed a state within the Arkonide Empire. They maintained only tenuous relations among themselves as long as conditions were peaceful but if a member was threatened by an outsider they closed ranks and rushed to his aid at once.

The Springers had become interested in Terra when the captain of the ship *ORLA XI* had observed in the Vega sector that somebody was engaged in substantial trade without regard to the monopoly of the Springers. Captain Orlgans had dispatched his agents to Terra and eventually captured an important prisoner – but only because Perry Rhodan had planned it that way. Rhodan followed the Springer ship and took it under attack. However, he became involved in a battle with a fleet of warships which suddenly came to the defence of their confreres. Realizing that it would be beyond his capability to withstand such superior forces for long with his three or four ships, Perry Rhodan journeyed to the artificial planet Wanderer, the abode of the hyper-brain, to obtain the newest and most formidable weapon, a teletransmitter. The hyper-brain – the quintessence of conscious souls of physically extinct race of yore – granted two transmitters to Rhodan for installation in his mightiest battleship, the *Stardust*, and no more. Thus Rhodan remained as technically inferior as before and had to use his wits to prevent the patriarchs of the traders from making strategic plans for the invasion of Terra at the Great Conclave called to convene for this purpose on Goszul's Planet.

The Springers had created a formidable military and industrial base on the Northern Continent after the patriarch Goszul had enhanced the retarding effect of the planet's environment. Accelerating the backward development by a factor of 10,000, he shaped a land which was inhabited mainly by natives with low intelligence. They induced the Gorrs, now named Goszuls, to accept a belief in Gods – and their Gods were the Springers themselves. They appointed robots as high priests and thereby exercised strict control over their lives.

Some of the more intelligent Goszuls were selected for a short hypnotic training with the aim of creating a cheap and humble workforce.

On the whole Goszul's Planet – or Gorr – was a living example of the fate which threatened Terra if the Springers ever succeeded in conquering it.

* * *

It was getting close to noon. Fafer had changed his course to a southwesterly direction.

Marshall and his team-mates had gone to the upper deck on a thorough inspection of the *Storrata*.

Szoltan had been locked up safely. He was allowed to move freely in a cabin but unable to open the door to the ship.

Marshall sat down on a coiled rope and studied one of the cannons on the deck. When he got up and took a few steps, he heard Tako Kakuta call him back: "Look out! Over there!"

Marshall crouched beside Tako on the boards and looked along his outstretched arm. He was glad to see three black points coming from the north close above the water's surface. "So they're coming after all," he exclaimed happily.

The sailor in the crow's nest seemed to have made the same discovery simultaneously. "Ship ahoy!" he shouted.

Fafer shouted back: "What is it?"

The lookout replied in a frightened tone: "Three vessels are approaching us from the north. They're moving above the water."

Marshall could see that Fafer was also alarmed. The sailors who had been close enough to witness the exchange of words murmured to each other:

"The Gods are coming in their flying chariots!"

Fafer was calm again. "Carry on!" his voice boomed across the deck. "We'll soon find out what they want."

Marshall gave his last minute instructions. "We'll stay here on the upper deck. I guess they'll send a man on board to negotiate with the captain. I don't believe they'll attack the ship since we've got a hostage on board."

The three craft approached rapidly. In spite of Fafer's orders the crew stopped all work. The men threw themselves down on the deck when the flying machines began to circle their ship. One finally hovered close enough to the middle deck to let a man step aboard.

"Kitai!" Marshall whispered. "Get down there!"

Kitai proceeded along the edge of the deck and cautiously walked down the narrow stairs to the middle deck. Marshall watched him take up a position, hiding behind a mast.

The Springer might have at first intended to talk to the captain but suddenly he changed his mind. Marshall saw him raise the portable radio to his mouth and talk into the mike.

The result became immediately apparent. The craft from which the man had disembarked landed on the deck and the second man climbed out. Then the second of the three machines took the place of the first near the edge of the deck and a third man emerged.

He joined his two mates and they stood together

on the middle deck, staring past the sailors who had meekly prostrated themselves.

"Tako!" Marshall gave him a terse order and Tako disappeared at once.

Katai Ishibashi waved his hand from behind the mast to Marshall as a sign that he had a firm hypnotic grip on the three Springers who had left their craft.

Nothing happened for awhile.

Then the machine into which Tako had teleported himself began to move. Slowly at first, as if the pilot at the controls was not familiar with the operation, the craft moved away from the ship and gained height, coming to a stop after a few minutes.

Marshall kept his eyes peeled for airships.

The craft hovering in midair suddenly loosed a disintegrator ray which hit the third vehicle, which was still circling the sailing ship. Half of the struck vehicle was dissolved in a swirling cloud of gas and the other half plummeted like a rock and hit the surface of the water with a loud splash. It sank without trace in three seconds.

Marshall and Yokida descended to the middle deck. The three Springers were still standing completely immobilized. They had failed to observe that one of their craft was shot down and paid no attention to the men approaching them, who had been joined by Kitai.

"Fafer!" Marshall shouted.

Fafer had followed the strange events with amazement and had come to the conclusion that his

72

passengers were far mightier than the Gods standing motionlessly on the deck. He came running,
eager to please.

"Listen, Fafer!" Marshall instructed him. "You
continue your journey to the Southern Continent.
Put these men on shore at the nearest island. You
don't have to be afraid of them – they're no Gods.
The moment they lose sight of your ship they'll
forget everything that happened to them. I promise
you that you'll never suffer the slightest punish-
ment. Do the same with the man we're holding
prisoner down there in the cabin. This goes also for
the Springer who'll leave the craft now coming in
for a landing."

Tako set the machine down on the deck. He slid a
few feet along its surface, none too gently nudging to
the side a few of the sailors crouching there.

He climbed out with a serious face. "I had to kill
him," he said gravely. "He tried to interfere with
me."

"You'll have only four prisoners in your cus-
tody," Marshall said to Fafer, trying to hide his
feelings of regret over the death of the Springer.

Fafer continued on the course of the *Storrata*
without change after the strangers had taken off
from his vessel in the two flying vehicles and
disappeared to the north.

* * *

Nothing except the thoughts of the crew indicated to Pucky that the little reconnaissance craft had landed. The antigrav-neutralizers absorbed all jars which without them would have been noticed in the ship's body while braking and touching the ground.

The crew got ready to leave the ship and so did Pucky. First he investigated the surroundings of the vast spaceport built by the Springers on the Northern Continent of Goszul's Planet. By teleporting himself in a far-ranging search he found a suitable hiding place in some nearby mountains for the equipment he had brought. He returned to the spaceship to perform the tele-transport.

As he had done 10 days ago on the *Stardust*, he made piece after piece of his baggage disappear. When he came to the last object, a heavy automatic disintegrator, the mishap occurred.

The telekinetic transport of articles required a high measure of mental concentration which could only be accomplished by breaking direct contact with the environment. Thus Pucky had no chance of noticing the maintenance robot who arrived on the corridor to check the condition of the ship after the crew had left.

Only a little accident – the fact that Pucky had to sneeze because of the dust raised by the equipment he so hastily removed – prevented him from transferring the automatic disintegrator to the hiding place.

At the same moment that Pucky was about to

finish his job after he sneezed, he felt a vibration of the floor.

He tried to determine by telepathy what was going on outside his room. However the attempt brought no results and before Pucky could take other measures the hatch to his little chamber slid open and a sturdily built robot bigger than a man came into view.

It was Pucky's good luck that the robot belonged to the category of repair machines and therefore reacted rather slowly and was not equipped with weapons.

Pucky went down on his forepaws and with lightning speed ripped open the contact seal of the water- and air-tight case in which the disintegrator was packed. The weapon was almost too heavy for the little mouse-beaver to lift the certainty that his mission would otherwise come to a premature end gave him enormous additional strength.

With a determined effort he raised the barrel high enough to aim at the centre of the plastic metal torso and violently pulled the trigger with his foot.

The shot dislodged a part of the robot's body, vaporized it and let the remnant of the machine crash to the ground in pieces.

Pucky dropped the heavy weapon back into its case, closed the contact seal and dispatched the disintegrator to the other packets.

Then he made a mistake.

The mistake: to assume that the absence of an

ordinary maintenance robot was not likely to be noticed very quickly.

Depending on his assumption, Pucky left the spaceship on all fours. He was certain that he would merely be regarded as a harmless animal if somebody were to see him. He carried only a small impulse-beamer for a weapon which he carefully hid in his fur. His spacesuit had been forwarded with the other baggage.

The limitless expanse of the spaceport seemed to be almost deserted in the bright light of the sun 221-Tatlira as it was called in the Springers' catalogue of stars.

There were many other ships but they were so far away from Pucky that only their upper halves were visible above the horizon.

The ships of the patriarchs were without exception of gigantic proportions. Yet from the distance they looked tiny and harmless.

Pucky toyed with the idea of teleporting himself on board a vessel and creating some mischief which would cause trouble for the patriarchs when they wanted to start up their spaceships. But he remembered his orders in time as well as Rhodan's warning: "So far the Springers don't know that the Terranian Spacefleet is involved in this action unless Marshall or one of his men couldn't keep their mouths shut. If anything happens to remind them of an incident on Snowman or in the Wanderer sector or anywhere else we've been, they'll quickly draw the right conclusions. So be careful!"

Regretfully Pucky discarded his idea. He was startled when he noticed a movement on the shimmering western horizon. He stopped and looked around. The same movement was discernible in the south, east and north.

Squadrons of little lens-shaped airships zoomed across the wide, smooth field and columns of robots were running behind them. It all went so fast that Pucky was virtually surrounded before he realized that the mighty array was staged for him.

He was the radial point toward which everything moved in straight lines, airships and robots.

They've registered the loss of the robot, Pucky thought.

And one other thought occurred to him at the same moment: some events must have taken place to make the Springers exercise unusual caution since Rhodan had last heard from Marshall.

Suddenly he became very curious to find out what Marshall had done in the meantime but he didn't care to linger much longer in his precarious spot.

He disappeared by teleportation before anyone could clearly recognize him or realize that he was the object of the search.

He landed in the vicinity of the hiding place where he had transported his entire material. Pucky had no illusions that the Springers would be satisfied to search the landing field and drop the search if they found nothing there. They obviously made a major effort which made it likely that their failure to detect the culprit in the spaceport would lead them to extend their operation to the surrounding areas and the present cache was located only a few miles from the eastern edge of the spaceport.

What made it worse were the microcoms. These sets were of the latest miniaturized design and were capable of bridging up to a couple light-years for direct audio-communications in spite of their compact size. But even when not in use they scattered some radiation due to the fact that the little energy cells were constantly collecting and storing energy.

Pucky was convinced that he wouldn't remain undisturbed for long at his retreat. But before the Springers would be in a position to close in on him he wanted to take care of a matter which was very important to him.

* * *

The flight proceeded without a hitch after the minor difficulties in the first few minutes due to their unfamiliarity with the operation of the strange craft. The two patrol ships neared the shore of the Northern Continent at maximum speed.

The land appeared to be very sparsely settled in this zone. Kitai finally discovered a little town which was situated near the shore and had a harbour about half as big as Saluntad. A few sailing ships were lying at anchor, proving that the simple natives maintained relations with their feared

78

masters in the Land of the Gods as they called the Northern Continent.

Marshall lowered his machine after he crossed the shoreline and ordered Tako Kakuta to follow him. The two craft hugged the ground, presenting only a tiny target for the rangefinder stations of the Springers.

Marshall flew by the seat of his pants. He had only the vaguest leads to the location of the place where the Springers had held their conference. The terrain below was completely foreign to him. The only detail he could remember was the fact that the huge spaceport where the vessels of the patriarchs were stationed was situated no more than 50 or 60 miles inland.

Forty miles north of the coast Marshall set his ship down. It would have meant stretching their luck to fly further.

They got out of the aircraft and abandoned them.

The terrain was sloped. Marshall began to recall that a low chain of mountains had been visible south of the spaceport. Perhaps it was the same mountain they started to climb and they would be able to see the spaceport once they had reached the ridge.

At dusk they decided to make camp. Tama Yokida had scouted a little valley with convenient exits and found what was important, water.

They slaked their thirst but were unable to still their hunger and deplored their lack of foresight in taking along some victuals.

Nevertheless they slept soundly and woke up late in the morning. They got up refreshed and eager to go on though hungry.

Marshall promised to shoot an edible animal with his impulse-beamer as soon as it was spotted and to roast it over a fire. "Besides," he assured his companions, "it can't be very far to the spaceport from here. As soon as we can see it Tako can zero in on their provisions. I believe the Springers like to eat well."

Marshall grinned and wanted to go on talking but he suddenly seemed to hear something. He stood still and the grin left his face. After awhile he relaxed again. "We've made contact with Pucky!" he called out. "He's close by!"

Kitai shouted joyfully but Tako was sceptical. "Are you sure?" he asked.

"Absolutely!" Marshall said emphatically. "He's no more than 30 miles north of us. He . . . quiet!"

Marshall listened once more. The others could hear him murmur something, giving telepathic answers supported by spoken words for better concentration. "Yes . . . we did a good job . . . 80% of all patriarchs killed . . . we're still considered to be men from the *LEV* . . . Yes, crew members of the *LEV XIV* . . . That was all, we had to scram . . . no, no other information. As far as we know the Springers didn't change their mind . . . but we can't be sure. Yes, you can pass the message on. But how? Microcom? OK."

Marshall turned around. "Rhodan is not very

far, boys!" he rejoiced. "Eight light-days away! Pucky is in touch with him. He's got some new-fangled audio set."

They were overcome by joy and gratitude and forgot their pangs of hunger. Marching as fast as the rough and dense terrain permitted they headed toward the place where Pucky was holed up with his crates.

*   *   *

By inclination and according to the letter of the law Etztak was an equal among the patriarchs.

The events of the last few days, however, during which it was proved over and again that Etztak's seemingly exaggerated caution was justified and those who believed that their safety wasn't seriously threatened turned out to be wrong, had caused the old man to assume a prominent role in the ranks of the patriarchs.

Now they listened to his opinions and began to study the suspicions voiced by him that the perpetrators of the disastrous attack belonged to the same people who had been discovered some time ago by Capt. Orlgans in a branch of the Galaxy. A suspicion which everybody had considered as asinine only a few hours ago.

Etztak was a very old man with rare intelligence. "The prisoners escaped again," he roared, making the two patriarchs Vallingar and Wovton standing next to him in the control room of his ship cringe as if they were personally responsible for this blunder.

"One of our most valuable agents was demolished and is useless. Our man was kidnapped, one craft destroyed and two others captured. Three men were killed and three more taken prisoner. And now at least one of the cunning intruders has landed right on our base in the *FRER LXXII* and we didn't find him."

"We didn't find him *yet*," Vallingar corrected him cautiously. "The search isn't ended yet."

Etztak made a disdainful gesture. "If he could vanish before our eyes from the face of the spaceport, how do you expect to seize him in the mountains where he can hide so easily?"

As if the technician in the communication centre had waited for this cue, the telecom began to hum just as Etztak finished his last word.

Etztak flipped the switch. "What's the matter?" he asked angrily.

"The search patrol has found something, Lord!" the man replied hastily and fearfully.

"What did they find?" Etztak shouted impatiently.

"A scatter of radiation in a five-dimensional region, but very weak. They don't know what the source of this radiation could be but they believe they have grounds for suspicion."

"Is that so?" Etztak sneered. "Tell those blockheads to land and investigate or they'll have to answer to me!"

The intimidated technician reassured Etztak that he would relay his orders at once.

Jubilantly Etztak, who had been only a few seconds ago of the opinion that the search would end in abject failure, turned to the two patriarchs. "All isn't lost yet! In a few minutes we'll have collared him or them."

* * *

Pucky was surprised by the unexpectedly quick success of the patrol ships. He had transmitted Marshall's information to Rhodan in a condensed scrambled message over the microcom and the call had been acknowledged.

As he carefully put down the set on the ground to pack it away again, he saw the shadow of the first aircraft glide over him. He fled a few feet to seek cover and looked around.

The ship was not the only one approaching his hideout. They came from all sides; 15, 20, 25. Pucky was in a trap. But his own safety was not endangered: he was able to save his hide by a teleportation jump even when his adversary stretched out his hand to snatch him.

But his real concern was his equipment. It was not only valuable but it would reveal to the Springers who it was that opposed them. And this had to be prevented by all means for the time being.

Pucky darted back from under his cover in the rocky mountain wall to pick up the microcom and its container. He quickly encased the set, returned to the other packages and extricated the automatic disintegrator again from its crate.

He started to transport the first bundles to a safer place. He remembered having observed the course of a river flowing through an impressive gap in the cliffs onto the coastal plain at the foot of the other side of the high mesa. The gorge was deep enough for Pucky's purpose. It provided a natural barrier to block the telltale radiation of the microcom from being emitted upwards.

Pucky had only a slight chance to get rid of the entire load before the Springers swooped down on him. Unfortunately he couldn't quite make it.

He crouched over the barrel of the heavy disintegrator and killed five of the Springers who had left their ships, in the meantime heading straight for his secret shelter with a guiding device in one hand and a weapon in the other.

Then he called Marshall.

* * *

Marshall was scrambling up a smooth precipice when Pucky's call reached him. The intensity of the call jolted Marshall to such a degree that he lost his precarious grip and slid down to the foot of the stone wall where his companions were waiting.

"Silence!"

Pucky's message was short and concise.

"Pucky's in trouble!" Marshall related quickly. "The Springers have cornered him and he doesn't want to abandon his equipment. He asks if Tako can find his way to join him."

Tako was ready at once. "Distance, reference points?"

"Distance approximately 25 miles, direction east-north-east. Identification mark: squadrons of aircraft in the air and on the ground."

"OK," Tako said and disappeared.

* * *

Tako landed six feet behind Pucky's back. Pucky operated the heavy disintegrator with some difficulty. At the moment Tako showed up, a greenish glowing shot whistled from the barrel and a few Springers trying to advance toward their positions met their death.

"Careful, Pucky!" Tako called out. "I'm here."

Pucky slowly turned around and showed his incisor. "I know," he lisped. "I didn't have time to say hello to you."

He pointed his paw to one of the grey bundles lying next to him. "Open it up and take out the impulse-beamer! These fellers aren't going to let us live in peace for some time!"

Tako complied in a hurry. Only after he held the weapon in his hands did he take time to survey the situation.

Pucky lay at the southwestern flank of a towering monolith shielded by a fow of lower rocks. The patrol-ship pilots seemed to know exactly where their opponent was. As they circled the big rock they ventured much closer east and north of the steep walls than elsewhere.

So far they had not had an opportunity to take a good shot at Pucky because Pucky's heavy automatic weapon reached at least as far as the cannons mounted aboard their little ships.

Covered by the lower cliffs Tako crawled with his impulse-beamer to the northern flank of the monolith. From a safe distance he aimed the barrel of his weapon upwards and turned five Springer ships into steaming plastic metal before the Springers caught on that this side of the crag had become perilous too and that it was time to retreat to a respectful distance.

Tako crawled back. The pile of goods beside Pucky had meanwhile been reduced. Pucky used every free second to launch another piece. Now he had only four packages left behind to be deposited under the surface of the river in the mountains.

"Sooner or later they'll realize that they're not getting anywhere," Tako commented as he watched the aircraft flying wide circles around the rocky peak, "then they'll bring in their heavy artillery to blast us out."

Pucky agreed eagerly. "I know. But I think we'll be done here before it comes to that."

One more of the four packages went phhht, followed 20 seconds later by another.

Then the Springers attacked once more. They had changed their tactic. From two sides – south and west – they stormed in on foot. Simultaneously half a dozen planes abruptly rounded both sides of the towering pinnacle, keeping close to the ground.

Had Pucky been alone this method of assault might have put him in serious jeopardy. As it was, Tako, took on the right half of the enemies and peppered their vessels with such an awesome fusillade that they turned tail in horror before they could do more than get off a few wild shots. Pucky worked over the other side with equal success. The Springers fled head over heels and it looked like Pucky would have a pause for a few minutes to finish his job.

He dispatched one of the last two pieces of their new destination and sent the two empty containers of the automatic disintegrator and Tako's impulse-beamer after them. Then he pointed to the last case and instructed Tako: "Take it to Marshall and come back. I hope I can hold out in the meantime."

Tako didn't know what the contents of the case were. It seemed to have special importance for Pucky. He took the case in his arms, memorized with closed eyes where he had left Marshall and his friends and took off.

Marshall didn't get a chance to ask questions. As suddenly as Tako had reappeared he vanished again and Marshall was left with an open mouth.

No change had occurred in Pucky's position. "They're still scared out of their wits," he lisped contemptuously.

Tako noticed in the background of the plateau a

few Springer ships taking off at a steep rate of climb in a westerly direction where the big spaceport was situated. He was willing to bet that the planes were on the way to request effective reinforcements.

"Of course you're perfectly right." Pucky's answer served to remind Tako that Pucky had not only mastered telekinetics and teleportation but was also a terrific telepath. "They went to get support but we'll be out of here by the time they get back and there will be nothing to fight against with their help."

Tako gave Pucky a precise description of the spot where Marshall was waiting. He jumped first and was amazed to see that his description had been so accurate that Pucky showed up a few seconds later only 30 feet away.

Marshall, Kitai and Tama welcomed him exuberantly and Pucky replied in his accustomed pert manner: "I wouldn't have come on my own volition but Rhodan told me to see whether those four hairy apes still happen to be alive by some accident and so I had to come!"

Finally they stopped bantering and took stock of their situation, which was far less rosy than they could have wished. The Springers had been alerted to their presence and to the specific incidents that occurred in their close proximity. It was a far cry from the vague manner in which they had reacted before. They expected the Springers to comb the entire Northern Continent with patrolships and to draw the mesh of the net so tight that there would be no reasonable hope of escape.

"We'll have to think up something clever," Marshall said in dismay, "and I mean soon."

* * *

Vallingar noted that Etztak was liable to apoplexy if he didn't soon calm down. He had never seen a man who could work himself into such a wrath as Etztak. With cracking voice Etztak screamed incoherently, at once cursing the pilots of the patrolships and the organizers of the search effort and finally the whole decadent race of the Springers.

Yet Vallingar really had to admit that Etztak had suffered enough provocation to raise his hackles.

Thirteen ships and 38 men were lost! And this in a fight with a foe who had not even shown his face. They didn't know who he was or how strong. The plane crews had reported at first that the defensive fire came from a single spot. But shortly thereafter they had lost five ships and their crews in a barrage from a different origin which made them change their opinion.

They had called for assistance with heavy weapons but before it arrived on the spot the men who had remained behind succeeded in storming the lair of the opponent without resistance. This would have been a wonderful feat if they could have nabbed their adversary. However the man or men who had put up such a formidable defence seemed to have vanished in thin air. The lair was empty.

That's why Etztak raged in awesome fury.

At the last minute – when he was still able to think clearly – Etztak had ordered all available ships to undertake a thorough and far-ranging search mission covering the entire continent and a vast area of the coastal waters. Then he went on his terrible rampage and kept ranting on and on without the least sign of a let-up.

Vallingar, who had been highly excited by Etztak's frenzy in the beginning, had now composed himself and watched Etztak's raving with curiosity, sitting in a comfortable chair.

The telecom buzzed and since Etztak in his wrath didn't pay the slightest attention to it, Vallingar effected the connection. The operator at the other end was visibly relieved not to see Etztak's red-mad face on the screen. "Two more ships reported destroyed, Lord!" he said with a sigh.

"Where?" Vallingar asked as calmly as he could.

The man stated the exact position of the shot down crafts. Vallingar verified it on the relief map covering a wall of the room.

Then he tried to snap Etztak out of his fit. He finally succeeded when he grabbed the robust old man by the collar of his cloak, turned him around and made him look at his face.

"They shot down two more ships," Vallingar said quietly.

Once Etztak's fury abated, he didn't lose his temper so quickly again.

"But now we know the direction in which our enemies have left," Vallingar added.

"Where . . . how?"

Vallingar dragged Etztak to the map and pointed to a big bright green spot. "Here our ships had the fruitless encounter with the strangers. And here," his hand shifted left toward a point midway between the green spot and the white rectangle of the spaceport, "the two aircraft were downed. Do you see?"

"Yes!" Etztak growled. "They're heading for the spaceport."

* * *

This was the "clever" ruse Marshall and Pucky had devised.

They needed a safe refuge as long as they received no further instructions from Rhodan and were the object of the Springers' methodical search.

Retreating to some place in a deserted region was considered to serve no purpose for them since the Springers were most certain to look for them in those areas right from the start and their chance of remaining undetected there was minimal in view of the drastic measures their pursuers were bound to take. They had better choose a place where the Springers were less likely to concentrate their efforts in the mistaken belief that it would be much easier to find them, namely a place among people.

The Springers figured that the fugitives would be clearly recognizable as members of the *LEV XIV* crew, for instance by the primitive sailors of the sailboats lying at anchor near the coast. If the idea occurred at all to the Springers that the fugitives concealed themselves aboard a sailing vessel they would simply make some inquiries by asking the captains of the ships a few pertinent questions. No captain would dare refuse to give a truthful answer to their "Gods."

For precisely these reasons they decided to seek shelter on a sailing ship, provided they could throw their pursuers off the track by planting misleading clues. The Springers had to be induced to believe that the hunted men took off in a different direction – to the spaceport, for example – so that they would pull back their search squads from all other parts of the Northern Continent.

This was the mission that fell to Tako and Pucky. Pucky had insisted that one of the heavy weapons remain with Marshall's group and gave the impulse-beamer to Marshall. Tako and Pucky armed themselves with the disintegrator besides carrying small rayguns in their pockets.

There was no doubt that their task was extremely risky. The moment they went into action they would have to face the full might of the hostile fleet. They had the disadvantage that they were unfamiliar with the terrain. Thus it was possible that one of their leaps would land them in the middle of a Springer formation and in such a case their chances for escape were virtually nil.

But it had to be done.

Marshall, Kitai Ishibashi and Tama Yokida sent off the two teleporters with rather uneasy feelings before they proceeded south to the coast.

*　*　*

The sky was darkened by swarms of auxiliary craft, flat bulky ground-to-ground transports used by the Springers as trucks, and smaller reconnaissance craft about the size of the *FRER LXXII* on which Pucky had travelled.

Tako and Pucky had slipped into a cave and waited to see what the Springers would do next. A few minutes earlier they had brought down two of their ships and, as expected, the whole armada dropped in from the skies.

However they gave their pursuers no clue to the presence other than the two demolished ships. Pucky and Tako emitted no such radiation as the microcom gave off that they had left with Marshall's team.

Tako checked his watch. Marshall had started out on his way to the coast one hour and a half ago and the closest harbour was about 60 miles away. With the intensive search they were conducting, the Springers must have found the two wrecks immediately. To give Marshall enough time to reach his goal it was essential to keep up their feint as long as possible.

"We must get to the other side," Pucky lisped.

The other side of the long valley stretching from east to west was a few hundred yards to the north and presumably outside the zone where the Springers suspected the attackers to be.

Tako agreed. He considered it advantageous to spring another stinging surprise on their antagonists from a different location.

They quickly leaped one after another to a point which they had predetermined as accurately as they could. They landed on a wide hillside strewn with stones and large boulders. Pucky, who came in second only 15 feet away from Tako, scrambled for cover behind a huge rock. They worked like a practiced team.

At the southern edge of the valley they could see the first Springer ship descend with circumspection and their crews climb out using even greater caution.

A few single craft periodically veered away from their formation and flew along the steep sides of the valley trying to find a trace of their quarry.

"How about helping them a little?" Tako suggested.

He supported his disintegrator on an angular rock and lined up the sight of his barrel. He took his time. It wasn't necessary to follow their flights. Sooner or later one of them was bound to get into his sight

It took only a few minutes before it happened. All Tako had to do was bend a finger and let go of the trigger. He accomplished what he aimed to do. The beam from his disintegrator – lasting only one tenth of a second – struck the small ship that had ventured too close and vapourized a section of its hulk. Tako could easily have blown the entire ship, crew and all, to smithereens but he was satisfied to put the aircraft out of action and see it reeling helplessly and losing height. It hit the ground very hard but Tako was sure that the crew survived the impact. Rescue squads instantly rushed to their aid from all sides. The rescuers looked excited and disturbed.

It was interesting to watch the reaction of the other Springer ships. One of the men seemed to have spotted where the shot came from and passed on this bit of knowledge. With a sudden determination which the Springers hitherto had rarely shown they abandoned the scene of their activity and turned their attention to the northern slope of the valley.

"Stormy weather in sight," Tako growled and picked up his heavy weapon. "Let's move to the west!"

A few seconds after they had given up their position the Springers detonated their first shells there.

* * *

After marching for three hours without being

molested Marshall and his two companions reached some kind of a road.

Marshall was carrying the impulse-beamer on his shoulder. The weapon didn't weigh him down very heavily because Tama Yokida lightened his load by applying his rare telekinetic power.

Marshall stopped to study some wheel tracks which lined the road.

"What's wrong?" Kitai inquired.

"Look at these tracks!" Marshall replied. "Do you think the Springers would allow the native Goszuls to roam the land this far from the coast? The shore must be at least 35 miles to the south."

Kitai shook his head. "Perhaps the tracks weren't made by Goszuls. Why couldn't the Springers have done it?"

"Because the Springers don't have wheeled vehicles. They're basically nomads roving through space and they dislike to land on a planet and do it only very seldom. They don't have any use for vehicles with wheels."

Kitai muttered, "Who else could it have been?"

Marshall shrugged his shoulders. "I don't know," he admitted. "We'll find out if we keep walking along the road."

They kept to the side of the road where the wheels had left only intermittent tracks. The deep ruts in the middle of the road made it difficult to walk. They continued their march for another 30 minutes, their curiosity remaining unsatisfied.

But then Kitai suddenly stood still and made Tama stop as well. "Listen!" he exclaimed.

Straining their ears they detected a clattering and hissing noise which seemed to come from the base of the foothills where they had wandered onto the road.

"Wow!" Marshall called out. "That sounds just like my grandaddy's first car!"

They remained still and waited. Not for a moment did the thought occur to them that a thing which made such pitiful wheezing noises could constitute a danger.

Eventually it came into view. It shot around the last bend in the road in a daring curve, ran too far out onto the grass and got stuck. The puffing died down but started up again a few seconds later with increased volume. The strange vehicle rolled slowly but surely through the grass, cutting a wide swath and returned to the road gaining speed again as soon as it was back on the tracks. Finally it rumbled toward the waiting men.

Marshall started to laugh. "Not my grand-father's jalopy ... it looks more like my great-grandfather's horseless carriage!"

Actually it had little resemblance to an auto-mobile. It was simply a flatbed wagon, about 5 by 10 feet, with a little motor mounted underneath and some kind of a mechanism which probably was designed to steer the front axle.

Three men who were doubtlessly Goszuls sat on the contraption but they were dressed quite differently from the people Marshall and his group had seen before.

Marshall didn't have to read their thoughts to recognize who they were: they belonged to the class of natives who were deemed by the Springers to be suited for a superficial hypno-training to create cheap workers, a euphemism for slaves.

They teetered proudly on their wondrous automobile and started with amazement at the three pedestrians who did their best to hide their amusement.

The driver of the vehicle obviously tried to bring it to a halt. He finally managed to stop his rattling conveyance after it careened far beyond Marshall and his men.

Marshall was able to understand the thoughts of the Goszuls. They took Marshall and the two Japanese as well for hirelings of the Springers, or "servants of the Gods" as the simple-minded Goszuls called them.

"*Kvogo?*" asked the driver after he had accomplished his difficult job. "Where are you going?"

He spoke Interkosmo with the same melodious intonation as the other indigenous people of Goszul's Planet.

Marshall didn't try to imitate his intonation. "To the harbour," he answered simply.

The Goszul was baffled. "On foot?"

Marshall recognized the doubts which were in the Goszul's mind. *Didn't the Gods have a vehicle to spare for them?*

"The Gods didn't have a car for us to use," he informed the Goszul. "Would you give us a lift?"

"You know very well that it can't be done," the Goszul regretted.

Marshall verified the instructions that the vehicle could carry only three passengers. He looked at Tama and whispered to him, "The car can't carry more than three people. Can you give us a push?"

Tama nodded and Marshall turned back to the Goszul. "How about trying it out? What do you say?"

Without waiting for a reply he clambered on the wagon. The driver was about to protest that his automobile would collapse as Kitai and Tama quickly followed Marshall without damaging his fragile contraption.

Marshall laughed. "You see you can do it! Go on!"

The Goszul wouldn't even think of it. Marshall noticed the suspicion entering his brooding mind.

"Who exactly are you? Why do you talk so strangely and what is the thing you're carrying on your shoulder?"

"I don't know," Marshall replied impassively. "The Gods only told me to take it to the harbour. They never confide in their servants."

The answer seemed to satisfy the Goszul. "But where do you speak so differently as you do?" he inquired.

"I come from a country which is very far from here," Marshall explained.

"Not from the Southern Continent by any chance?" The Goszul's eyes lit up.

Marshall neglected to read the brain of the inquisitive man and simply answered: "Yes."

He instantly realized that he had made a mistake.

"That's where I'm from!" the Goszul exclaimed. "We're fellow countrymen . . ." He hesitated and narrowed his eyes. "But then I can't understand why your speech sounds so odd."

Marshall was about to give a long explanation about his fate and his travels which had taken him to many countries but before he could open his mouth the Goszul waved his hand and said: "You know, I could have the wrong impression. Your way of talking is really not that peculiar." With these words he turned around and started up the motor.

Marshall looked at Kitai who grinned roguishly. "Thank you! He was beginning to get difficult."

Kitai had allayed the suspicions of the Goszul by suggestion.

Marshall was curious about the motor powering the vehicle. After the driver had started it up Marshall listened to it closely and had no doubt that it was indeed a combustion motor of the type of gasoline engines. The smell of the fuel didn't remind Marshall of anything he had ever inhaled before but that didn't mean much: after all, a combustion engine can be run with alcohol too.

The most amazing aspect was really something else. The Springers, who were strictly space travellers and completely disinterested in rolling vehicles, had gone to the trouble of inventing something like an automobile for their servants. They probably didn't dare let the Goszuls use more efficient machines than these primitive, poorly functioning combustion engines.

Did this mean that the Springers didn't feel safe in the presence of the hypnotically trained Goszuls?

Marshall probed the thoughts of the three servants of the Gods but detected no hint that they resented the Springers. However this proved little because the men were not even thinking of the Springers at this moment.

In the meantime Tama Yokida had achieved the task of making the vehicle lighter so that the coughing motor was able to pull the lead. The driver was astounded by the speed at which his old crate bounced down the road. He turned around and announced happily: "We'll be in the harbour in three hours!"

* * *

The weird battle had shifted farther north. Tako guessed that they were at the same latitude as the northern border of the spaceport. It was time to move to the west.

The intermittent fighting had so far cost the

Springers five auxiliary ships and two air transports and all they had to show for it in their reports to their superiors was that they never failed to find the position of the hostile gunners after the first shot and yet were always beaten by a nose when they arrived on the spot.

A panic began to spread among the searchers. These weren't normal fighters – they were ghosts!

However Etztak screamed in a new outburst of his ire that he would punish by death anyone retreating from the search before the enemy was caught – dead or alive.

* * *

Four and a half hours had elapsed since their separation from Marshall. Tako figured it would take at least four times that long till Marshall reached the harbour. Till now Tako had not learned that Marshall had been able to commandeer a vehicle.

The town looked quite different from Saluntad. They couldn't see a single house which compared to Vethussar's residence in the south.

However it possessed a harbour where three trans-oceanic sailing ships were lying at anchor. The ships were big enough to hide an entire company of Terranian guerrilla fighters.

Suddenly Marshall was in a hurry to get off the motorized cart. It was apparent at first glance that there were numerous Springer robots present in the town and as long as they didn't know for what purpose they were here they had to reckon with the possibility that one of them might decide to check up on the passengers of the clattering automobile and that no suggestion could deter them from their task, only the force of weapons.

Marshall expressed his thanks to the three Goszuls and promised to return the kindness if the occasion should arise. Then he quickly departed with his friends. The driver was baffled that his vehicle responded again in the same cumbersome old way although his load was greatly reduced.

Marshall got off the main street, which had the heaviest traffic and where most of the robots appeared to congregate. They kept walking along a side street which seemed to lead into the direction of the harbour.

Marshall considered sending a message to Pucky that they had arrived at the harbour earlier than expected. But fortunately he didn't have enough time to use the microcom to carry out his intention.

Out from another side street crossing the lane along which they were walking, a group of metallic robots rounded the corner with noisy clanking steps.

Marshall looked furtively around. There were several other people in the streets who had also noticed the robots but paid no further attention to them and so Marshall decided it would be best to behave in the same disinterested manner. He continued walking as closely along the houses in the

103

lane as the barrel of his impulse-beamer allowed him, staring straight ahead in the air as if he had other problems on his mind.

However the robots were unwilling to let the three men pass without further ado. When they had come within 20 feet the first robot stopped and the other three lined up at his side blocking the narrow lane completely.

"Halt!" one of the robot's rasped, "It was you who arrived in town on the last wagon, right?"

It took all of Marshall's aplomb to face the inquisitive robot squarely. Looking him up and down, he replied: "Yes, but it's none of your business!"

The onlookers who had hoped to watch an amusing spectacle reacted in a characteristic manner. The lane was deserted in a trice. Everybody scrambled to get behind the nearest house door. Only the four robots and the three Earthlings were left in the lane.

"What's this thing you're carrying?" the robot insisted, disregarding Marshall's inciting remark.

Suddenly it flashed through Marshall's mind: *the microcom!* Pucky had warned him that it emitted radiation. The robots had registered it automatically.

Well, Marshall resignedly thought, *at least we know it's useless trying to pull the wool over their eyes.* "I don't know," he replied with an expression of indifference.

The electronic brain of the robot made an

instantaneous decision with its customary built-in efficiency. "Follow me!" he ordered.

Without another word he turned around and marched back down the lane. The three other robots remained in their position till Tama had passed them by last and then formed the rearguard.

Marshall was aware of the chances he took by following the order and he whispered to his comrades in English: "We'll hold our fire till we get to a lonely neighbourhood. We don't want witnesses!"

They understood his reasons. If necessary Kitai could have ordered two, three or even four witnesses to forget what they saw but more than that would have been too difficult under the circumstances. A tumult caused by the news spreading through town that four robots were destroyed was the last thing they needed.

Obediently they trotted behind the leading robot and avoided looking behind at the three robots marching in the back.

The first robot turned into the street from which he had come and Marshall saw with pleasure that farther away toward the southeast the houses were getting sparser. If they could get as far as that without being incarcerated by the robots the battle was as good as won.

* * *

Tako blasted another machine out of the sky, watched as it plunged down to the ground and was ready to make a jump. By now the Springers had learned to react to each attack with utmost swiftness.

But this time it was different. Tako waited for the machines to swoop down on him but they remained where they were.

For a while anyway. Then they regrouped, zoomed into the sky, flying southward over the next mountain chain, and disappeared.

Tako grinned. "They must have something new up their sleeves, hey?"

He couldn't know that Etztak had talked a minute ago with the port of Vintina and that the pilots of the search commando had received new instructions.

Pucky lisped: "I don't understand it!" Shaking his head he was about to add something but at the same moment his eyes widened with a blank stare as if he were listening to something. When he returned to normal he was rather excited. "Marshall and his men have been captured in the town by robots. I didn't get it all but they seem to be in trouble. We've got to go there at once!"

Marshall had fairly well described where the town was situated. There was nothing to hold them here and so they took off on the spot.

*　*　*

The robots didn't have the slightest intention of accommodating Marshall. Long before they reached the few houses at the end of the street the robot ahead of them made a turn and opened the door of a house which looked just as dirty and shabby as the rest of them in the neighbourhood. He motioned his prisoners to enter the dark hall behind the door.

Marshall didn't think twice. He didn't know what fate awaited them in the house. It could very well be a trap from which they might have great trouble extricating themselves.

Better to risk a tumult in the town!

"Look out!" he warned in English with an expressionless face.

The door was low. Marshall acted as if he had to take the impulse-beamer off his shoulder to be able to pass through the door. The weapon smoothly slid down under his arm and he already had his finger on the trigger when he suddenly whirled around.

Tama and Yokida had caught on. They kept out of the line of fire and Marshall played the hissing white beam on the first robot, mowing him down before he knew what happened. Steaming metal flowed onto the ground, spreading an unbearable heat, and solidified in a grey puddle.

The two Japanese withdrew farther to the side and Marshall wiped out two more of the robots, who apparently lacked orders to go into action. The last one, probably responding to an emergency signal, reacted just at the moment that Tama and Kitai figured that the small guns they carried in their pockets could be used as well against the

107

machine. The two needle-thin energy beams penetrated the head enclosure and set the robot swaying.

Marshall took care of the rest.

Meanwhile it had become so hot that their hair was singed and their clothes began to smoke.

"Let's get out of here!" Marshall gasped. "To the right!"

Right was where they had come from. Marshall reacted instinctively. Although he didn't know the sympathies of the population, he felt it would be safest to hide in a crowd, the bigger the better.

He had no doubt – after he heard Pucky's story – that the Springers learned about the demolition of their robots at the same moment they were obliterated.

The street was empty. As Marshall ran down it he could see here and there a frightened face. A panic was rampant among the inhabitants of Vintina. It probably was the first time anyone had dared defend himself against the robots.

Marshall calculated the question in his mind as to how long it would take the Springers to take countermeasures after the extermination of their four robots. Would they have enough time to reach the harbour and find refuge aboard one of the ships?

At the pace they were running it was 10 minutes at the most to the harbour. To find a ship and to persuade the captain by hypnosis to refrain from objections to boarding his ship under suspicious circumstances would require another 10 minutes, perhaps as many as 15.

If the Springers delayed their retaliatory actions for the destroyed police machines by half an hour, their margin would be acceptable.

But otherwise?

* * *

Tako and Pucky landed near the outskirts of the town. They watched the fleet of auxiliary ships, air transports and other smaller vessels of the pursuers descend and spread out over the city. Scores of ships set down in the cramped lanes and spewed out their crews.

Tako intercepted one of the low flying transports with his disintegrator, threw it into a spin and made it crack up on the ground.

A part of the fighting force cruising over the town was ordered back and resumed the hunt for the gunners lying in ambush at the outskirts.

The same game which had taken place during the last few hours up in the mountains was repeated again. Tako and Pucky fired and leaped away, fired and leaped away. In this manner they succeeded in drawing away three-fourths of the armada while the rest concentrated its search on the area of the town. If Marshall managed to elude the pursuers for a little while longer, the Springers would sooner or later gain the impression that the assassins of the robots had already slipped away and were identical with the people harassing and annihilating their forces outside the town with virtually no fear of retribution.

Pucky advised Marshall of his strategy. Marshall received the impulse and consented.

*   *   *

It took the Springers no more than 15 minutes to take the first steps in their counteroffensive. Marshall heard a whirring in the air, glanced up while running and noticed a round auxiliary ship crossing the street over the rooftops.

The street along which they were sprinting led straight to the port. At the end of the street they discerned the hull of a ship – almost close enough to touch.

Just as Marshall was wondering if it wouldn't be smarter to duck into some hide-out till it became clearer what the Springers were up to, three of the small auxiliary ships appeared from the harbour and touched down in the street.

Their hatches opened up and some heavily armed Springers debarked. They were still too far away to arouse the suspicion of the three figures. But they advanced along the street and came so close that it was bound to draw their attention if Marshall and his pals suddenly turned around and fled in the opposite direction.

"Caution!" Marshall whispered. "Duck into the nearest house!"

It was at this moment that Marshall received Pucky's message. Marshall acknowledged it and added hastily: "We're going in hiding right now!"

110

Tama tried to open the door of a nearby house. The door was barred. Tama wanted to open the door by applying his telekinesis but he needed some time for concentration. Marshall grabbed him by the shoulder and pulled him to the next house. "It'll take too long!" he grunted.

Three of the Springers had approached within 300 feet. If the next house door was also locked it was time to start shooting. Kitai would be unable to force the three men to obey his will quickly enough.

Tama jiggled the odd triangular doorknob, pulled and pushed with all his strength and shook the door, making the old wood groan. To no avail.

"Get behind me!" Marshall ordered. "Let's put up a good fight!"

Tama and Kitai complied and put down the microcom. Kitai began to concentrate so he could assist Marshall at the critical moment. The distance between them and the detachment was still too great for effective suggestive influence.

Marshall slowly raised the barrel of his thermo-beamer from the cover of the doorway.

Then and there the door behind them opened slowly, a small crack at first. A hand slipped through the crack, seized Tama's arm and pulled him inside as the opening widened.

Kitai followed willingly after alerting Marshall and picking up the microcom. Finally Marshall retreated to the safety of the dark hallway and the door was shut.

"Down to the cellar!" a strange voice commanded.

Something squeaked. Tama, who had preceded them in the corridor, remarked: "There's a door and steps behind it."

"It's no use," Marshall answered. "The Springers have seen us withdraw into this house. They'll . . ."

Outside the feet of the Springers were pounding the cobblestone pavement and came to a stop in front of the door. Marshall heard the twisting of the doorknob but apparently it had been bolted again as before.

"Open up!" a hoarse voice shouted.

"Whoever you are," Marshall said to the unknown man in the darkness, "you better open the door or they'll burn your house down! We'll be able to take care of ourselves."

The man retreated down the corridor with shuffling feet, passed Marshall and reached the door.

"Tama, down the stairs!" Marshall ordered. "Kitai, see what you can do with them. If necessary I'll handle them myself."

Kitai gave no reply. He was already at work. The cautious patter of Tama's feet could be heard moving down the stairs. A cold draught of air came from somewhere.

The housedoor swung open and the light outlined the small skinny figure of the stranger against the dark.

112

He bowed low. "Oh, what an undeserved honour . . ." he began to murmur.

But one of the Springers interrupted him brusquely. "You're hiding three strangers in your house. Unhand the fugitives of the law!"

The thin man straightened up again. "How could I? You're saying this in jest to the lowest of your servants, Lord!"

"Stop your blabbering! I'll . . ."

Another Springer put his hand on the speaker's shoulder and whispered something in his ear as he turned his head.

"You really think so?" he asked with furrowed brow.

A moment later he also became convinced of the same idea which Kitai had already suggested to his two companions, namely that there had never been any strangers in the street and therefore they were never seen by them.

"What are you gaping at?" he barked at the little man. "Shut the door and get back to your work!"

The scrawny figure bowed a second time and obeyed.

Marshall took a deep breath as the steps outside faded away.

The man shuffled back. "You treat the Gods with most uncanny might!" he chuckled. "It pleases me to have helped such worthy people."

"What caused you to help us?" Marshall inquired.

"You've killed four machines of the Gods," the

113

other replied. "This is the best reason to be grateful to you and assist you any way I can. All my people feel the same way as I do but they've got more to lose and are therefore afraid to aid you. Don't you want to go down the stairs?"

"No, not any more," Marshall answered. "We must go to the harbour. Perhaps we'll be lucky this time and get through."

"Perhaps," the man chuckled. "But if you go down the cellar you're sure to be lucky."

Marshall had a fleeting feeling of suspicion but the plastic metal of the impulse-beamer in his arm reassured him. What could the little man do against him? "Well, then," Marshall decided, "let's go down!"

Kitai carried the microcom and groped in the dark for the top of the staircase. Then he descended, followed by Marshall. The native was last.

Tama called from below. "I wish it weren't so dark in here. I can feel some cold air coming in."

The little man giggled again. Marshall stepped on smooth ground and then heard a crackling and a weak light flickered behind him. Their host had kindled a torch.

They were in a cellar room which wasn't very big. It had one unusual feature: a circular opening in one of the walls about three feet high.

The little old man with dirty dishevelled hair in ragged clothes pointed to the hole. "Through there," he said with a titter. "The hole ends at the pier, the width of a hand above water. If the tide comes in, the passage is half full. It's inclined toward the harbour."

Marshall read his thoughts. His information was correct. "We thank you," he said earnestly. "We'll remember you, Wosetell, at another time."

The old man gave no sign of surprise that Marshall knew his name. He answered gravely: "You've shown how powerful you are. I believe that some day you'll be able to mete out the same fate to all these evil gods as you've done with their four machines. But don't lose any time, each second counts!"

Tama crawled into the opening. Kitai handed him the microcom and followed. Marshall nodded to the old man and entered the hole after Kitai's shoes were no longer visible.

Wosetell kept chuckling behind them.

Marshall seemed to be in luck.

After one hour the Springers had come to the conclusion that none of the escaped men still tarried in the town's district and they concentrated their efforts on those locations where well-aimed shots continued to flash, decimating their patrols slowly but surely.

Tako and Pucky teleported themselves a few hundred yards farther north with each jump. The Springers were completely vexed. They either faced the same enemy with whom they slugged it out in the mountains – then it was impossible to understand how they had so quickly arrived on the scene without visible means of transportation

– or they were dealing with another foe, then it was implausible that they would expect to get near the spaceport under the watchful eyes of the defenders as the first group of intruders had attempted.

Tako surmised that the Springers were wrestling with these problems and wondered how long it would take Etztak to realize that he was not confronted by crew-members of the *LEV XIV* but by his most implacable enemies.

The weird battle continued shifting farther to the north.

The Springers persuaded themselves more and more that their quarry must have left Vintina. They knew that four men of Levtan's crew had escaped. The detachment that harassed their armada so unmercifully certainly consisted of no less than four men.

Marshall reported that he and his two men had boarded a ship and that they had brought the whole crew including the captain under sub-conscious control. Pucky sent his answer. "O.K. We'll join you as soon as we've drawn the Springers far enough away from town."

* * *

Taking over the *Orahondo* had not been very difficult. The ship was anchored only a few feet from the exit of Wosetell's secret passage to the pier. They left the microcom and the impulse-

116

beamer in the passage, swam to the ship and climbed aboard using a rope.

The crew of the ship belonged to an ingenuous class of Goszuls. Kitai had little trouble moulding their thoughts in such a way that they accepted everything very obligingly that best served the safety of the three men and their absent friends.

Kitai paid special attention to the captain with the result that he housed them in three comfortable cabins and promised to prepare two more cabins for the two friends whom they expected to arrive a little later.

As soon as they were alone in the privacy of their cabins Tama Yokida telekinetically hauled the impulse-beamer and the microcom aboard.

Marshall reported the success of their operation to Pucky and at this moment he and Pucky were startled as they received an intense impulse of unknown origin: "Who in the world is talking there?"

Pucky recovered from his surprise quicker than Marshall. "What was that?"

"It was I!" came the mysterious answer.

"And who are you?" Pucky continued his query.

"I'm a servant of the Gods!"

"It's a telepathic Goszul, Pucky!" Marshall interjected a warning. "He could be dangerous!"

"I know," Pucky replied. "Wait a minute!"

Pucky's next impulse was directed to the Goszul: "Will you do us a favour, my friend?"

"That all depends."

"I'll explain it to you. We're involved in some important business and if you keep interrupting us you'll ruin our transactions. If you agree to keep silent until we've concluded our business we're willing to offer you a share of our gains."

The reply was tinged with sarcasm. "You can't conceal your thoughts from me, stranger, no matter how hard you try. You're an enemy of the Gods, aren't you?"

Pucky perceived that the unknown Goszul was really able to fathom his innermost thoughts to a dismaying degree. Since deception was impossible, he answered truthfully. "That's right," he admitted.

"Then I'll keep silent," replied the Goszul. "Any enemy of the Gods is a friend of mine!"

Marshall probed the impulse intently. It was, without doubt, genuine. The Goszul meant what he expressed mentally.

There seemed to be more enemies of the Gods biding their time in this land than appeared on the surface.

Pucky sighed with relief . . . if a lisping sigh can be imagined.

*   *   *

Two hours later Pucky and Tako had reached the harbour of Vintina and there boarded the *Orahondo* in one mighty leap from the southern border of the spaceport.

The captain and crew of the ship had been

mentally prepared for the peculiar visitor which was Pucky. There would be no complications, no cause for concern, no reason for any of the sailors to pass on the information to the Springers, for Kitai had done his job exceedingly well and the hypnotic prohibitions he had installed were more restrictive than steel barriers.

Marshall recapped the events of the past few days, then sent a highly condensed version to Perry Rhodan via microcom.

Rhodan's answer came promptly: "The Springers' Northern Continent base must be razed in the shortest time by guerrilla warfare and without assistance from our ships."

Marshall read the microcom's tape-printed message with unbelieving eyes. "We're supposed to wipe out their base?" he choked incredulously. "How – with our bare hands?"

Pucky bared his incisor as he twisted his face into a familiar grin. "You forget the stuff I'm holding in reserve in the river. It's enough to blow up half the Galaxy . . ."

"Tsk, tsk, tsk!" Kitai snickered.

"Well, enough to annihilate this ridiculous base, anyway!" Pucky revised his estimate slightly downward.

Marshall sighed. "And I thought all we had to do was hang around for a few days till Rhodan came to get us. Now the whole rigmarole starts all over again!"

Pucky, for once grave, observed seriously: "It's

not that bad. We're getting a rest for the time being. The Springers haven't the slightest notion we're still in Vintina and aboard the *Orahondo*. They're busy ruining their eyes looking for us in the mountains around the spaceport. Now that we've attracted their attention away from us the time is most opportune to launch our offensive."

Tako Kakuta remarked thoughtfully, "Maybe we ought to devote some time to the local inhabitants – the 'servants of the Gods' and the primitives. I've got a feeling that a clandestine organization of resistance is already in existence. If this is true we won't have to start entirely from scratch."

Marshall smiled wanly. "OK – here we go again! But there's one thing I'd like to know: when is an officer of the New Power old enough to retire?"

"Why, did you have somebody specific in mind?" chirped Pucky. Then, with a mischievous glint in his eye: "Perhaps you're wondering if *you're* eligible? You do seem pretty old for such important work."

"Huh? Who! Me, old? Retire and miss all the fun? I thought you could read minds, Pucky. You sure you aren't getting senile?"

"Senile!" Pucky snapped back. He was so rattled that his tongue got in the way of his eyeteeth and he couldn't see what he was saying till he had blurted it out and everybody was dying with laughter:

"Me! Senile! *I'm too old for that!*"